NO LADY
FOR THE LORD

Daughters of Desire
(Scandalous Ladies), Book Two
A Sweet Regency Romance

COLLETTE CAMERON

Blue Rose Romance®
Portland, Oregon

Sweet-to-Spicy Timeless Romance®

NO LADY FOR THE LORD
Daughters of Desire (Scandalous Ladies)
A Sweet Inspirational Regency Romance
Copyright © 2021 Collette Cameron®
Cover Art: Jaycee DeLorenzo—Sweet' N Spicy Designs

Attn: Permissions Coordinator
Blue Rose Romance®
8420 N Ivanhoe # 83054
Portland, Oregon 97203

eBook ISBN: 9781954307964
Print Book ISBN: 9781954307971
collettecameron.com

Other Collette Cameron Books

Daughters of Desire (Scandalous Ladies)
A Lady, A Kiss, A Christmas Wish
No Lady For The Lord
Coming soon in the series!
Love Lessons For A Lady
His One And Only Lady

Check out Collette's Other Series
Castle Brides
Highland Heather Romancing a Scot
The Blue Rose Regency Romances:
The Culpepper Misses
Seductive Scoundrels
The Honorable Rogues®
Heart of a Scot

Collections
Lords in Love
The Honorable Rogues® Books 1-3
The Honorable Rogues® Books 4-6
Seductive Scoundrels Series Books 1-3
Seductive Scoundrels Series Books 4-6
The Blue Rose Regency Romances-
The Culpepper Misses Series 1-2

Dedication

For every woman who has smiled when she wanted to cry

&

prayed when she had no hope.

*I am so happy to learn of your marriage to
Doctor Morrisette. My wholehearted and sincerest
felicitations to you both. Thank you for the invitation
to tea. I should have adored seeing Purity, Trinity, and
Faith once again. It has been so very long since we
ere all together at Haven House and Academy
for the Enrichment of Young Women. However
I regret that I shall have to beg off this time.
The household is in mourning, and I cannot
leave my orphaned charges.*

~ Miss Mercy Feathers in a letter to
Mrs. Joy Morrisette

Rochester, England
Residence of the now-deceased Lieutenant Lewis
Masterson
20 February 1818
Late afternoon

A torrential sheet of plump raindrops pinged ruthlessly against the leaded-glass panes partially concealed by lace curtains and the heavy draperies festooning the mullioned windows. The floral brocade's warm, comforting hues of jade, poppy, gold, pewter, and ivory complimented the cinnamon and saffron striped overstuffed chairs and divan situated near the fireplace.

Surrounded by tufted and tasseled brocade pillows and with a fat, extremely spoiled cat sprawled across her lap, Mercy Feathers and her devastated young charges cuddled on the sofa.

Angry wind gusts pummeled the swaying trees and thrashing shrubs outside but had little effect against the sturdy, seven-decades-old, four-story brick house—other than rendering an occasional jarring, hair-raising rattle to a glass pane.

More than once in the past hour, a particularly fierce blast had battered the house, startling Mercy. Naturally, she endeavored to conceal her discomfit but had quite seriously wondered if the windows could withstand the continued violent onslaught.

Behind a gold-scrolled screen, a robust blaze crackled and hissed merrily within the green-tiled fireplace. Gleaming from frequent polishing and the flickering flames, the carved black walnut mantel framing the hearth stood regal and proud as it had for years.

And yet—Mercy skated a furtive glance about the room—a cloying chill permeated the somber, well-appointed salon this afternoon. A chill the exuberantly snapping and sizzling blaze couldn't altogether eliminate. A chill which, truthfully, had more to do with the room's grief-stricken occupants than the petulant weather currently engaged in a toddler's tantrum outdoors.

The pungent, almost sickening aroma of lilies in the many vases of conciliatory bouquets situated throughout the salon overwhelmed the comforting, familiar odors of beeswax, linseed oil, and burning maple logs.

Six weeks of smelling the blossoms' pungent odor had become tiresome.

Just when Mercy believed she'd be granted a reprieve from the choking fragrance, more flowers arrived from another well-wisher, having only just learned of the lieutenant's untimely death from lung fever.

So help her God, any further bouquets would be sent directly to the rubbish bin.

Unless they were carnations or peonies. Mercy would never tire of those blossoms' subtler essences.

"Golden slumbers kiss your eyes," she sang ever so softly to the girls huddled against her.

"Smiles await you when you rise.

"Sleep, pretty babies, do not cry,

"And I shall sing a lullaby."

Exhausted, Mercy rested her head against the back of the divan and stared up at the intricately molded plasterwork. A single gossamer cobweb had escaped the diligent maids' notice and dangled from the ceiling. The strand lazily rotated 'round and 'round as if taunting her, challenging her to rise from her comfortable seat and swipe it away.

A wry, nascent smile edged the corners of her mouth upward a jot.

That was not going to happen.

She was too blasted tired and too dashed comfortable to make the effort. Besides, she'd disturb her young charges.

With her gaze, she followed the twirling thread downward until her attention came to rest upon the fire's soothing snapping once more. Rain lashed the windows, and the flames fluttered and sputtered against a blast of wind hurtling and howling down the chimney.

A shiver scuttling across her shoulders, Mercy glanced outside. The storm—the wickedest in her memory—showed no signs of abating.

That same slate-colored sky had opened and spilled its contents as Lieutenant Lewis Masterson's glossy cherry-wood casket was gently lowered into the unsympathetic, cold black earth. The heavens had wept nonstop for four long days afterward, as had the sable-haired little girls now curled trustingly against Mercy.

They were much too young and innocent to experience such loss. Much too young to understand their lives would soon be subjected to more upheaval.

God, comfort these precious orphans. Give them peace and strength, Mercy prayed silently.

She wouldn't mind a generous portion of both virtues as well.

In the month and a half since the serious but kindly former naval officer had shuffled off his mortal coil and been laid to rest, the rain had continued to relentlessly pelt Rochester several days a week. Miniature streams trickled across the already saturated greens, made muddy rivulets in the gardens, and wended, serpent-like, over the circular brick courtyard.

Sorrow, dread, anxiety, uncertainty, and no small amount of fear romped about Mercy's insides, causing waves of nausea to ebb and flow. Churn and tumble.

Over and over and *over*.

Acrid bile billowed up her throat, and she swallowed—hard.

I think I'm going to be sick.

This same despair and unease had overcome her often of late.

Specifically, since the lieutenant had died and she'd been forced into the role of managing his household. Even to the point of using her small savings to keep food on the table and pay the faithful staff half wages. She couldn't afford to pay them more.

So far, only two servants had departed.

Cammie Sumner, a surly chambermaid who dawdled about more than she actually worked, and Silas Bottoms, a shy stable hand, had lasted only a week without full wages. When offered a promotion to a groom's position at a neighboring estate, Silas had bashfully approached Mercy and resigned his position.

She'd been sorry to see the sweet, bumbling Silas

leave but understood. He was supporting an invalid mother and two younger brothers. Mercy had genuinely wished him well.

However, she had been less reluctant to see the back side of the disgruntled maid. Hired nine months before the lieutenant's death, Cammie Sumner was lazy, gossiped incessantly, and resented working. Her parents owned one of the local inns, and she considered herself well above the lowly station of a mere chambermaid. Furthermore, her tart tongue and slatternly behavior were grounds for dismissal.

Mrs. Stanley, the cook and the closest thing the Mansfield House had to a housekeeper, had to regularly chastise Cammie about her sloppy work, her frequent woolgathering, and for making doe eyes at the lieutenant.

Thrice, Mercy had to remind Cammie that it was most improper for her to openly flirt with the man. To which the maid had snarled that Mercy was merely jealous because she wanted Lieutenant Masterson for herself.

The preposterous suggestion had never crossed Mercy's mind, and to hear a maid vocalize such claptrap had raised her temper. She'd told Cammie Sumner exactly what she thought of her ludicrous accusation and that, if serving girl entertained such vile considerations, it would be best for her to tender her resignation.

Her hopes of becoming Lieutenant Masterson's

mistress dashed, Cammie had taken herself back to The Hair of the Hog's Pub and Inn exactly seven days after his death.

Good riddance to bad rubbish.

Thank goodness the lieutenant had either been oblivious to Cammie's simpering or a superb master at masking his emotions, for he'd never indicated he'd noticed her coy and less than subtle antics.

No more servants had complained at their reduced circumstances or left to find employment elsewhere. *Yet.* They would, though. What was more, none of the staff would be guaranteed their positions after *the guardian* barged into their tranquil tableau.

She closed her eyes for a long blink and marshaled her equanimity.

Now wasn't the time to entertain feckless feminine weaknesses. Arabelle and Bellamy needed her to remain stoic. Calm. Focused. Mercy was their steadying rudder in this riotous sea of confusion and fright in which they'd been cast and had absolutely no control over and little understanding of either.

Regardless, Mercy was heartily sick of the rain. And dank. And gray.

Gray. Gray. Gray. Everywhere, rotted gray.

Shades of gray from pale dove to ominous charcoal cloaked the sky, the grounds, the horizon, and, yes, even the interior of the once cheery but now inarguably gloomy house.

Mirrors had been turned to face the walls, an

ebony cloth hung over Lieutenant Masterson's portrait, and black wreaths adorned several doors. To honor the deceased, fewer sconces and lamps flickered throughout the house, thereby filling the corridors with weird shadows and a tomb-like miasma. Fewer tapers were also an economizing necessity.

Even the crisp black gowns, stockings, shoes, and hair ribbons Mercy and the girls wore contributed to the dull, lifeless atmosphere and made their faces appear ashen and drawn. Such was commonplace in a household after the death of the master. However, this oppression was made much worse by the ambiguous futures of the sniffling orphans plastered to her sides.

Another contentious rumble of thunder shook the sturdy four-story brick manor. Unlike the bleating wind, those heavenly tremors *did* have the ability to jangle more than just the windows. Namely, Mercy's nerves.

Boom! Boom-boom-BOOM!

Gasping simultaneously, Arabelle and Bellamy burrowed closer to Mercy.

"Miss Mercy. I'm scared," seven-year-old Arabelle sobbed, clutching Mercy's arm while her trembling, almost nine-year-old sister huddled low on the divan, hands clasped over her ears.

"Shh, darlings," Mercy pacified, drawing them nearer and running her hands in soothing sweeps over their quivering shoulders. She told them what Mrs. Hester Shepherd, the proprietress of Haven House and

Academy for the Enrichment of Young Women, had always told the discarded girls in her care. "You're quite safe, my dears. I promise. It's just the Good Lord rearranging his furniture in heaven to make room for more souls."

How many times had Mercy told them that nonsensical twaddle which had worked to calm her childhood fears?

She'd barely finished speaking before another deafening explosion clamored overhead, and vivid blue light flashed beyond the windows.

Even the cat, Fluffer-Muffer, flicked her long silvery tail and twitched her black-tipped ears, though she didn't deign to bother opening her bottle-green eyes. It would take something much more catastrophic than thunder and lightning to stir her from her comfortable snooze.

Arabelle had wanted to name the cat—acquired four years ago as a fat, wriggling spitfire of a kitten—Fluffy. Bellamy, however, had insisted the feline should be named Muffin. Hence, after much discussion, a few unkind words, and more than one bout of frustrated tears, a compromise of Fluffer-Muffer had been reached.

As much as the pampered puss enjoyed the girls' doting attention, the cat's heart had belonged to the lieutenant. More often than was comfortable, some unfortunate vermin or bird—and, *God forbid,* the occasional snake—had been laid proudly at his booted feet as the feline blinked adoring green eyes up at him.

Whenever Lieutenant Masterson was away, a broken-hearted Fluffer-Muffer prowled the house yowling for him. Often, she could be found curled atop his bed, awaiting his return.

A half-smile edged the corner of Mercy's mouth upward.

Countless times she had searched the house looking for the naughty puss so Mercy could deposit the cat in the nursery for the night.

Lieutenant Masterson had never been able to quite get the cat's unusual—*clever*—name right—or so he repeatedly exclaimed. He'd lower his chin to his chest and deepen his voice to a theatrical rumble while reciting an assortment of ridiculous names.

Fluffingmuff? Flutter-Mitten? Mossy-Muffin? Moldy-Muffin?

Of course, he'd been jesting.

Nevertheless, his silly antics had sent his daughters into fits of giggles, as was his intent. He'd been a good father—patient, kind, and loving. And fun. That he'd picked a stranger, a man unknown to the girls, to act as their guardian came as a surprise to everyone.

In fairness, Mercy reasoned, what other option did the lieutenant have?

"Miss Mercy?" Bellamy's muffled voice came from the vicinity of Mercy's underarm. "Please keep singing," she begged in a watery, quavering voice pitched higher than usual. "It's not so awfully scary when you sing."

"Of course, darling." Mercy resumed singing the lullaby where she'd left off.

"Cares you know not, therefore sleep,

"While over you a watch I'll keep,

"Sleep, pretty darlings, do not cry,

"And I shall sing a lullaby."

Mercy had slightly altered the song to include both girls rather than a singular child as the serenade was written.

Storms had terrified the sisters before Mercy, at nineteen years of age, had become their governess five years ago and moved into the chamber next to the nursery. Many were the nights the girls had clambered uninvited into her bed. Then, as they did now, the three of them snuggled together, and Mercy sang lullabies and hymns while a tempest seethed outside.

This might very well be the last time she comforted Arabelle and Bellamy during a storm.

How can I bear it, God?

Joy wrote me about your unfortunate circumstance,
Mercy. Please accept my deepest condolences,
my dear. We, women, are at the mercy of providence,
are we not? I've discreetly inquired of Balderbrook's
Institution for Genteel Ladies if there is a need for
another instructor. Your French and dancing were
always far superior to every other girl at Haven
House and Academy for the Enrichment of Young
women. Sadly, at this time, there are no openings.
I shall not give up, however.

~ Miss Chasity Noble in a letter to
Miss Mercy Feathers

2

Still the residence of Lieutenant Masterson
20 February 1818
Later that stormy afternoon

Sighing and blinking back the tears burning hotly behind her eyelids, Mercy touched her cheek to first one girl's silky chestnut head and then the other—Lord, how she loved these precious little girls. So much so that her heart cracked a little more each time she thought of their impending separation. A good, solid shake of the house might send the fractured organ now beating in her chest scattering all over the floor.

Not only had Mercy taught Arabelle and Bellamy everything, from which fork to use at dinner and how to divide fractions, but she'd also mothered the girls. Kissed their bruises, combed and plaited their hair each night, dried their tears, and celebrated their milestones.

She fretted about their uncertain futures.

Hers as well, truth be told.

Her position was no longer secure, and Chasity Noble, an instructor at Balderbrook's Institution for Genteel Ladies, had written that there were no openings at the school in the foreseeable future.

Lieutenant Masterson had no living relatives, and the guardian he'd appointed for the girls had been an officer he'd served with in the navy.

At least that was what the prune-faced, sour-breathed solicitor had explained in his condescending twang a week after the funeral. A horrid little scarecrow of a man, Joseph Bralen, Esquire, had all but implied that Mercy had been the lieutenant's long-time mistress.

"As your particular...*services* are no longer required, Miss Feathers," he'd said in haughty disparaging tones, "you should prepare to depart the residence the instant the Masterson girls' guardian sends for them."

Renewed outrage warmed Mercy's blood in a way the roaring fire never could.

How dare Mr. Bralen make such a vulgar insinuation?

Lewis Masterson had never stopped loving nor grieving over his beloved wife. Not once had he ever addressed Mercy with anything other than the respect and propriety her position required.

Neither was Mr. Bralen in a position to terminate her employment, the presumptuous, mean-spirited toad.

Glancing down, first at Bellamy and then at Arabelle, Mercy gave her head a slight shake. Worry proved a burdensome mantle that only weighed more as time passed. Reciting scripture and praying as she'd been taught as a child by Mrs. Shepherd alleviated only a portion of her unease.

A frown knitted her forehead as she puzzled through the questions haunting her days and nights these past weeks.

What is to become of us now?

Who was this guardian?

What kind of man was he?

Was he married?

What if…What if he refused the appointment?

Heavens above.

Mercy's heart tripped over an irregular beat at the unbidden thought before resuming its steady rhythm. She wrinkled her nose in consternation. That disagreeable possibility wasn't altogether farfetched. The newly appointed guardian wasn't a relative, and many men wouldn't welcome having two young girls foisted upon him.

Especially if he were a rakehell or rogue.

She also fervently prayed this mystery man from London would still need a governess for the girls. However, he might have children of his own and therefore not need her services. Or—she cringed at the disturbing thought—he would choose to send Arabelle and Bellamy to a boarding school.

At once, Mercy banished the horrible notion to the ash pile. He simply could not. It was unconscionable. To do so would destroy these sensitive girls. She would tell him so herself if the opportunity arose.

Meshing her lips together, Mercy considered her few options if the new guardian discharged her. Over the past five years, she'd saved most of what she'd earned.

Unfortunately, she'd learned how expediently a household of this size burned through funds. The merchants and grocers that had always extended credit to the lieutenant until the end of each month were reluctant to continue doing so without a guarantee of prompt payment.

She couldn't blame them, though their distrust stung.

Mr. Bralen hadn't thought to release any monies for salaries or foodstuffs either. Most inconsiderate of the uptight, judgmental man. But as she'd been obligated to use her savings to keep food on the table, her financial position wasn't as secure as it would otherwise have been. She didn't begrudge the necessity, and she intended to ask this enigmatic guardian for a reimbursement.

However, as Mercy knew very well, there was no legal requirement for repayment.

She supposed she could return to Haven House and Academy for the Enrichment of Young Women, the foundling home where she'd been raised, until another position could be acquired. Even so, everything in her railed at the unwelcome thought.

To return after five years like a disgraced prodigal son?

Well, prodigal daughter in her case.

More critical and equally disturbing was how could she bear the separation from Bellamy and Arabelle? She'd come to love them as if they were her own daughters.

That, naturally, had been foolish.

In fact, she'd been cautioned not to do that very thing.

Hadn't Mercy been instructed on punctuality, poise, professionalism, and, above all, to never allow sentiment to dictate? She was to perform her duties with diligence and proficiency and ensure an employer had no cause for complaint or criticism.

But Mercy was never, *ever* to become emotionally attached to her charges. They were hers for a season in her life and theirs. They and she would move on.

It was the way of the gentry and nobility.

Naturally, Mercy had done everything expected of

her professionally but forbidding her heart to love the little girls entrusted to her care all day, every day, for years and feel nothing for them?

No, it wasn't possible. Only a heartless ogre could resist loving these precious girls.

Arabelle and Bellamy needed the love Mercy gave them, and she couldn't regret inviting them into her heart, even if it meant despair now.

Of course, she was fully aware the day would come when the sisters would no longer need her. But that day had been *years* away. She would've had time to prepare herself and them for the inevitable parting. By then, they would've been young ladies, intrepid and confident, and ready to make their own way in the world.

Well, as much as it was possible for gently bred young ladies to steer their own course, given society's ever-present restrictions on females.

At least they weren't illegitimate, as was Mercy. That zealously guarded secret was known only by the plump, kind proprietress of Haven House and Academy for the Enrichment of Young Women and the other discarded daughters of illicit desire who called the facility their girlhood home.

Another sardonic smile skewed her mouth sideways.

And, of course, whichever of those female children's anonymous parents had seen to her placement at the exclusive home.

Sparing another disinterested glance out the window to the rain thrashing the courtyard, Mercy wondered again for the umpteenth time when they'd hear from the negligent guardian.

Just over six weeks isn't so long, she reminded herself.

It certainly was when she worried about finances and the sisters' futures.

She tightened her embrace around the girls.

Mercy hadn't wept upon the lieutenant's death, nor did she consider herself a watering pot. But the notion of never seeing these drowsy darlings nestled trustingly against her filled her eyes with stinging tears.

Her throat worked spasmodically as she wrested her sentiments under control. Swallowing the obstruction that had formed in her constricted throat, Mercy took three calming breaths.

One—inhale, exhale slowly.

Two—inhale, exhale slowly.

Three—inhale, exhale slowly.

Yielding to her tumultuous emotions was neither productive nor wise.

Any hint of weakness on her part would spear uncertainty and dread in the girls who already fussed about what was to come. Neither girl remembered their mother, and now that their father had passed, Mercy was the only adult remaining in their lives.

Except for the devoted servants, but that wasn't the same.

The girls had been utterly inconsolable at the loss of their beloved father.

Even now, damp spots marred Mercy's bombazine gown from their recent bout of tears.

She troubled her lower lip, alternating her attention from the fire, her charges, and the doleful scene beyond the window. The storm appeared to have blown itself out or moved farther away. The rain had slackened, as had the wind.

Waiting. Waiting. Waiting.

Weeks without a word back from the girls' new guardian—Lord Ronan Brockman. Mercy only knew his name, not what his naval ranking had been. She presumed from the "Lord" before his name that he was a younger son.

Irritation welled at his inconsideration. Perhaps his lack of response meant he didn't mean to accept the guardianship after all. Mr. Bralen hadn't specified what happened then, but Mercy felt confident the consequences wouldn't bode well for the girls.

Mayhap she ought to take matters into her own hands and write this Lord Ronan Brockman formerly of his Majesty's Navy and make inquiries herself.

The idea wiggled around in her mind for a few blinks and then took root.

Mercy straightened on the sofa, disrupting Fluffer-Muffer's slumber.

Dare she?

The cat gave her a one-eyed "What are you

doing?" insipid glance before closing said eye once more. Less than a blink later, soft feline snores joined the fire and storm's chorus.

Do I dare?

Yes? *Yes!*

The more Mercy thought about it, the more the idea of writing to Lord Ronan Brockman had merit. Surely his address was contained somewhere amongst the lieutenant's will and the rest of the information Mr. Bralen had deemed necessary to leave.

Those papers still lay undisturbed atop Lieutenant Masterson's desk.

Why hadn't she considered this before?

It made perfect sense.

Mercy could introduce the girls to their guardian—explain their likes and dislikes and their valid concerns. She could pave the proverbial way for Arabelle's and Bellamy's transition to a new life. Help to smooth that change.

Who better, in truth, than Mercy to do so?

That dried prune Mr. Bralen hadn't cared about the girls' feelings. He'd simply said to have them packed and ready to go at a moment's notice, constantly referring to them as the *Masterson girls*. Like they were inanimate objects without feelings to be loaded onto a freight cart.

What if Ronan Brockman is just as uncaring?

If he ignored her missive, then she'd have to consider alternate plans. However, nothing this side of death would keep her from helping Arabelle and Bellamy by whatever means she could.

Mercy set a disgruntled Fluffer-Muffer on the floor and stood.

Tail swishing, the cat arched her back in irritation and made little chirping noises. Her sign that she was well and truly miffed.

"I'm sorry, Fluffer-Muffer. You'll have to find another place to doze other than my lap."

With a haughty flick of her tail, the imposed upon feline minced to a nearby chair and jumped onto the cushion.

No creature was capable of a greater silent put down like a miffed cat.

Reaching a hand out to each girl who glanced up at Mercy quizzically, she squeezed their fingers. "I need to write a very important letter, darlings. Could you entertain yourselves in the nursery until I am finished?"

Clasping hands, they nodded in unison, their big, cinnamon-brown eyes brimming with curiosity.

"Might we have warm milk and biscuits?" Bellamy asked, generally the bolder of the two.

Her younger sister nodded eagerly, sending her dark ringlets pirouetting. "Oh, yes, please, Miss Mercy."

"I think that can be arranged," Mercy said with a smile. The first genuine smile in weeks, and her cheek muscles ached from non-use.

Neither girl had demonstrated much appetite since their father's passing, and if they hungered for a treat before dinner, Mercy wasn't going to squelch the desire.

After accompanying them to the kitchen and making the request for milk and biscuits from the ruddy-cheeked cook, Mrs. Stanley, Mercy gave each girl a warm hug.

"Go along with you now. I'll be up as soon as I've finished my correspondence, and we can read *Gulliver's Travels* together. I've asked for toasted cheese and soup for our supper. I think we'll don our nightwear and eat before the fire, picnic style."

Mercy leaned back and examined each of their dear faces. "Does that sound like fun?"

"Yes," they responded in unison, both carefully balancing a plate of biscuits and a cup of milk.

Even as she promised to return soon and strode to the study, Mercy's mind had moved on to composing the letter. Would it be too forward or presumptuous to ask when Lord Ronan Brockman intended to meet the girls before he sent for them or if he required a governess?

What could it hurt to ask?

She might get sacked for impertinence.

Honestly, she might get sacked regardless. Better to know the lay of that land as swiftly as possible too.

Giving a slight lift of her shoulder, Mercy settled into the oversized leather chair behind Lieutenant

Masterson's desk. She pulled the documents, left there that blustery January day six weeks ago, across the slightly dusty surface.

With the slightest hesitation, prudence still niggling that she overstepped the mark, Mercy examined the tidy rows of script crossing the vellum. Not finding what she sought on the top page, she continued perusing each crisp page until she located the one with the information she wanted.

Aha. Success.

"Lord Ronan Brockman," she muttered beneath her breath as she copied his direction in neat, even letters. A dashed lord and quite possibly a rapscallion. Nevertheless, it was unfair to judge a man she'd never met. "I do hope you are a man of good character and have a benevolent heart."

Patience and a sense of humor wouldn't be amiss either.

The letter took a surprisingly short amount of time to complete. After rereading each line carefully, Mercy blew on the damp ink. Lips pressed together, she took a deep breath as she sprinkled sand across the foolscap.

"Why pray tell, Lord Rogue, haven't you had the common decency to reach out to your grieving wards yet, you bounder?"

I know I have thrust an unexpected and inconvenient burden upon you. I beg your forgiveness even as I implore you to accept the appointment. I didn't expect to die before my daughters were grown. However, if you're reading this letter, then I am no more. Ronan, there is no finer person on earth, other than their governess, who I would trust Arabelle's and Bellamy's care to than you.

~ Lieutenant Masterson in a letter to
Lord Ronan Brockman
Included with Lieutenant's Last Will and Testament

3

Mayfair
London, England
The lodgings of one extremely exhausted Lord Ronan Brockman
26 February 1818 - early morning

ap. Rap-rap-rap.
R "Sod off," Ronan mumbled sleepily, his face mashed into his pillow. Burrowing further into the comfortable bedcovers, he drifted back into slumber's welcome embrace.

Rap. Rap.
"My lord?"

Ronan pulled a pillow over his head. He couldn't have been asleep more than an hour or two. Every limb felt weighted with lead, and for certain, someone had stuffed his head with wool. Dirty, wet wool.

Rap. Rap. RAP.

The last knock rattled the door and jingled the lock.

Bloody persistent bugger.

"'Tis Pillington, your lordship."

Blister and blast.

Groaning, Ronan flopped onto his back and covered his eyes with a bent elbow.

What in Hades was one of Father's footmen doing here?

One thing was for absolute certain. The loyal servant wouldn't go away until he'd delivered whatever message he'd been sent across London at— Ronan raised his arm and squinted at the table clock— seven of the clock to do so.

Father must be in fine fettle to send for him at this deplorable hour.

Rap. Rap. Rap.

"My lord?" An edge of impatience had crept into the dutiful servant's voice. "Your father requests your presence straightaway."

Not just a message then, but a royal summons. By none other than the Marquess of Trentholm himself. One did not ignore such a directive and not suffer unpleasant consequences.

Heaving a resigned sigh, Ronan sat up. He shoved the bedcovers aside, then yawned widely, raising his arms overhead and stretching.

Rap. Rap-rap-rap. Rap-rap-rap. Rap-rap-rap-rap-rap.

Sounded like a demented woodpecker.

Despite his exhaustion, Ronan chuckled.

"I'm coming, Pillington."

Groggy from lack of sleep, he swung his bare legs over the edge of the bed. Standing on the clothing he'd unceremoniously discarded less than three very short hours ago, he raked his fingers through his hair.

Catching sight of his naked form, he grinned. He had best throw on a banyan, or he'd shock the staid footman. It would serve Pillington right for waking him if Ronan flung open the door naked as a robin.

Yawning again, he shrugged into the jade and black striped silk robe. Tying the garment loosely at the waist, he strode to the door, his bare feet slapping on the wooden floor as the silk swished around his ankles.

He threw the panel open, and with his forearm braced against the doorframe, he cocked a lazy grin.

"Yes, Pillington?" Ronan couldn't quite keep the drollness from his tone.

Well trained, the disciplined servant's gaze never drifted below Ronan's nose.

"The marquess requests your presence straightaway," he repeated unnecessarily. "A coach awaits you outside."

Of course, it did.

Father left nothing to chance. Ever.

For instance, Ronan climbing back into his comfortable bed for a few more hours of much-needed sleep before putting in an appearance at Pelandale House's study. Which, most likely, would be a full-on interrogation.

Why couldn't his sire be one of those lazy slugabed aristocrats who lounged in bed until noon?

No, the fifth Marquess of Trentholm rose at the wholly ungodly hour of five each morn.

Every bloody morning.

Before the birds or the sun arose.

Who did that unless forced to, as Ronan had been obliged to do during his stint in His Majesty's Navy?

Ronan shuddered in horror.

Oh, mornings were fine. *If* one had slept enough the night before—which he most certainly had not— but he preferred rising at seven himself.

What was more, his sire was so blasted cheerful upon rising that one either wanted to plant him a facer or wonder what he'd imbibed to make him so impossibly jolly.

People were not supposed to be jovial in the morning.

"I don't suppose there's coffee in the coach too. And milk?" Ronan couldn't resist goading, knowing full well there wasn't. "Bacon? Biscuits? Sausages?"

Zounds, he'd missed good ol' British sausage.

"No, sir," Pillington answered in complete seriousness, his bland expression not so much as twitching. "But you may partake at breakfast."

One day, Ronan was going to get this veritable perfection of a footman to crack a smile.

Ten pounds to the first person who made Pillington laugh outright.

Ronan eyed the stoic fellow, his mien an impressive neutral mask. Hmm, better make that twenty pounds.

"Permit me fifteen minutes," Ronan said.

He ought to be able to manage a half-presentable personage in a quarter-hour.

However, he'd be buggered if he'd shave for this interrogation or whatever this command constituted. If his father dragged Ronan from the first comfortable mattress he had slept upon in the past two-and-one-half months, then by thunder, he would show up bristly-faced as well as baggy-eyed.

Mayhap he wouldn't even cleanse his teeth.

He ran his tongue over the back of them and grimaced. On second thought, his mouth felt like a herd of mud-covered cattle had rolled around inside. A good cleansing was definitely in order.

"Very good, my lord," Pillington said, taking a step away. "I shall await you at the coach."

With a brusque nod, Ronan shut the door.

Pillington would return in precisely fifteen minutes and begin hammering upon the door with the diligence of a carpenter if Ronan were a second late.

After swiftly performing his morning ablutions—sans shaving—he donned his clothes. He grinned at his reflection in the mirror. If Fickel—Father's valet—saw the travesty of fashion tied haphazardly around Ronan's neck, he'd expire from apoplexy.

Ronan's grin took on a wicked slant as he deliberately pulled the neckcloth farther askew and unbuttoned two buttons on his coat.

Standing back, hands on his hips, he perused his endeavors.

Ah, perfect.

Roguish and rumpled and just slightly rebellious.

He'd be bound if Father or Sanford, the Earl of Renshaw—Ronan's   older-by-almost-three-years brother—would comment on his unkempt appearance before Ronan had downed his first cup of much-needed coffee. Though it stretched the bounds of one's imagination, Sanford was impossibly stuffier and more pompous than their father

If Benjamin, the youngest Brockman brother at seven-and-twenty, was present, however, he'd give Ronan a cocky salute and make a ridiculous inquiry about whether he was wearing undergarments, had applied bear oil to style his short hair, or some other equally inappropriate query.

Benjamin was the opposite of Sanford in every possible way, from Benjamin's fair coloring to his easygoing, jocular temperament. Ronan fell somewhere in the middle, which was why he was oft' called upon to act the peacekeeper between his two vastly different brothers.

Their half-sisters, Corrina and Marissa, resembled their mother—Ronan and his brothers' stepmother— from the marchioness's ashen curls to her pale blue eyes. Whereas Marissa possessed her mother's calm, gentle temperament, Corrina possessed the fieriest temper of all of the Brockmans.

Concealing a wide yawn behind his hand, Ronan pulled the door shut on his rented rooms with the other. He blinked wearily, his eyes gritty and dry from too little sleep.

Lord, he was bloody tired.

He hadn't climbed into his somewhat inviting bed until the first rays of dawn shamelessly flirted with the horizon.

Why in God's holy name was he being beckoned at this hour?

More on point, how had Father even known he'd returned from the United States? The ship had only dropped anchor early this morn.

A wry grin tilted Ronan's mouth at one corner.

Father knew *everything*.

A mouse didn't fart in Pelandale House without the estimable Marquess of Trentholm knowing.

Likely, he'd had someone watching the docks for days in anticipation of Ronan's return.

That wasn't unusual.

Father kept close tabs on all three of his sons. Not only because he was controlling and commanding, which being a marquess, he was, of course. But because he also genuinely cared about his heir, spare, and third son.

Naturally, he worried over his two cossetted daughters, but the majority of their care he left to his wife's competent hands.

Even at nearly thirty, being the middle son and having been sickly as a child, Ronan received the greatest percentage of his father's...not precisely fussing, but definitely interference and concern. Never mind that Ronan had served as a sub-lieutenant in His Majesty's Navy for six years and survived the *Nightingale's* sinking.

He traced a fingertip the length of the scar running from his left ear, over his jaw, down his neck until the thin, jagged line disappeared into the hastily tied folds of his lopsided cravat.

In point of fact, he was lucky to have survived.

Many—*too many*—had not.

A hazy image blocked his vision, and the paneled corridor faded away to that fateful day and the horrors he'd tried to forget: The screams of the wounded and dying. The deafening blast of cannon fire from the pirate ship. Acrid smoke. Searing heat. Agonizing pain. Agony so overwhelming, he'd begged for death.

He was one of only eleven men able to escape. They'd spent days crowded into a single lifeboat floating in the North Atlantic Sea with no food and little water.

A new camaraderie—more profound and more meaningful—had sprung up among those survivors. When one faces death with someone, it changes one— melds men together on a primal level and in a manner difficult to express with words.

Eventually, a Dutch cargo ship had spotted their small craft bobbing in the icy sea and rescued them. Most of the sailors left the navy within a year or two of that disastrous event, but they'd stayed in touch, nonetheless.

Not regularly, however.

For men, at least those he was acquainted with, weren't the best at correspondence. Nevertheless, occasionally, a letter found its way to him, and sporadically, he'd respond. Lieutenant Lewis Masterson had arranged a few reunions, and every man who'd survived the *Nightingale's* sinking and who also still drew breath made a point to attend.

Sadly, at their last meeting, their number had dwindled to eight. Time and age offered no partiality to any man, lowborn or high. Rich or poor. Decent or depraved. Each eventually faced his Maker and was held accountable for his actions and words.

Giving himself a mental shrug and shaking his head and shoulders to dispel his dark reverie, Ronan made his way through the shadowy corridor, down the narrow stairwell, and out to the waiting coach. As always, the conveyance shone like a well-polished stone.

Praise God it was February, and no blaring sun blinded him, worsening his already pounding head. Lack of sleep always had that effect on him. Until he slept it off, the drums echoing inside his skull would continue to thunder mercilessly.

As Ronan approached, Pillington promptly opened the coach door.

Still pondering why his father couldn't have waited until a more hospitable hour to demand his second son play attendance upon him, he gave the servant a sardonic upward bend of his mouth and climbed inside.

Breathing out a long sigh, Ronan stretched his legs out before him, relaxing against the plush claret-colored squabs. After lowering his hat, he closed his bleary eyes. He dozed the entire twenty-minute ride to Pelandale House in Grosvenor Square and awoke with a start when the coach door opened.

A brisk blast of damp air slapped his face.

A fitting homecoming.

Ronan, how desperately I wish you were in London. I could use your advice, brother. I've met someone. Someone exceptional, and I know with absolute certainty that our pompous elder brother, and likely Mother and Father as well, will heartily disapprove.

~ Benjamin Brockman in a letter to
his brother, Ronan Brockman
Sent but never received

Grosvenor Square, Mayfair
London, England
Pelandale House - home of the very impatient Marquess of Trentholm
Slightly later in the morning, but still too bloody early

"**M**y lord, we have arrived," Pillington intoned with the same degree of enthusiasm a bored student might recite the Prince Regent's genealogy for the past five centuries.

Ronan shoved upright and sighed, pushing his hat atop his head.

He pinched the bridge of his nose for a long moment, hoping and failing to ease the persistent tempo pounding unmercifully in his noggin.

Best to get on with it.

The sooner he'd satisfied whatever it was his sire required, the sooner he could find his mattress again. If he'd slept more than four hours in a row on the merchant ship during the return voyage from America, he'd sing an aria this Christmastide.

Which was to say, he had not slept more than four hours sequentially at any given time and, therefore, would not impose such an atrocity on humankind.

Ronan did not have a singing voice.

In truth, he was tone deaf as a tree trunk and, as a kindness to the world at large, had long since ceased even so much as humming. Ironically, he could play the pianoforte quite well, but that was only because he either read or memorized the music.

Ever diplomatic, Pillington stood to the side, looking directly ahead.

"Thank you, Pillington."

Ronan had scarcely reached the top riser before the front door opened, and Sturges bowed.

"Welcome home, my lord," the butler greeted warmly, his eyes twinkling with genuine affection. He'd never addressed Ronan as lieutenant, even when he'd been in the navy.

"Thank you, Sturges. It's good to be home."

The thought of enjoying one of Mrs. Cullen's hearty breakfasts made Ronan's mouth water. He hadn't eaten a decent sausage in months, nor bread pudding.

"His lordship awaits you in his study," the butler said, accepting Ronan's hat, though he avoided meeting his eyes.

The study?

While Pillington's countenance remained smooth as a stone under every conceivable circumstance, Sturges's eyes gave away his every thought.

What the blazes was going on?

Puzzling his forehead, Ronan cast a longing glance down the corridor toward the dining room. There, he knew, an assortment of delicious foods lay spread upon the sideboard.

And coffee.

Strong and hot. Just the way he preferred. A beverage he desperately needed *now* if he were to keep his wits finely tuned for the verbal sparring that lay ahead with his sire.

"I'm to meet with Father before I break my fast?"

As Sturges closed the door, still studiously averting his gaze from Ronan's, he gave one solemn dip of his square chin. "I believe the matter is of some urgency."

Matter?

"Very well." Disregarding his aching head and his rumbling stomach, Ronan turned in the study's direction. "Might I request coffee be brought? I've had but three hours of sleep."

If that.

The servant dipped his silvery head again, a

36

knowing glint in his wise, gray eyes.

Ah, there was the Sturges of old.

"I've already requested a breakfast tray and coffee, sir," the servant said. "With your permission, I shall check on its progress."

"By all means." Nodding, Ronan smiled.

He wouldn't starve after all.

Would it be unacceptable to ask the elderly man to sprint to the kitchens?

Sturges strode briskly down the corridor, leaving Ronan to make his way to the study alone.

Why did he feel like a lad in short pants being called to task over an unknown infraction?

After giving the study door a single rap, he pushed it open and poked his head inside. He came up short upon seeing his mother, brothers, as well as Corrina assembled. Only Marissa was missing, and at sixteen, she must've been too young to take part in whatever *this* was.

Zounds.

Something truly serious must be afoot for almost the entire family to be assembled at this early hour.

"Ah, Ronan." His father glanced up and, a wide smile wreathing his face, beckoned Ronan inside. As was his wont, only a brightly colored waistcoat—today's was jade and primrose—interrupted the severe lines of his black suit. "Welcome home, Son."

Sanford took after their father in that regard, except Sanford would rather chew cow hooves than don anything so bright as green or yellow. Any hue other than a sedate gray and black striped waistcoat or, if he were feeling exceptionally bold and dashing, dark blue paisley.

"Do come in, my boy, and take a seat." Still smiling, Father gestured to one of the empty wingback chairs before his desk. "It is wonderful to see you."

"You as well, Father." He might be overbearing at times, but Ronan loved his father. "My ventures in America were successful," he added, knowing his father would ask that next.

"Good. Good." Hands resting on the arms of his chair, the marquess nodded. "Diligence always pays a decent return. You're amassing a respectable fortune."

Pride glinted in his sire's eyes, and Ronan couldn't help the swell of contentment billowing in his chest at his father's approval.

"Welcome home, darling." Resplendent in a lavender and ivory morning gown which accented her hair and eyes to perfection, Mother extended her hands and angled her lightly powdered cheek for a kiss. "I've missed you so, Ronan. It's just not the same when you aren't in England."

"I've missed you as well, Mother," Ronan responded automatically.

He had, in truth—quite a lot.

Rachael, Marchioness of Trentholm, was the only mother Benjamin had ever known. She'd been an affectionate and kind stepmother to all three Brockman boys. Only three years of age when his mother died, Benjamin had begun calling Rachael Mama within weeks of Father marrying her.

It had taken Ronan a while longer, but he had called her Mother for many years now as well.

Sanford still called her Stepmama, but that was a huge concession for the stuffy bore.

"You are looking very well, Ronan," Corrina declared, giving him a cheeky smile before rucking up her ocean blue gown and draping her calves over the arm of the chair she sat in. Toying with a tendril of pale blond hair, she swung her legs back and forth, revealing her prettily embroidered white stockings and not so dainty slippers.

The Brockman women had rather large feet.

So accustomed were his family to Corinna's hoydenish behavior—*is hoydenish even a word?*—no one remarked upon her unladylike conduct. Forcing social constraints upon Corrina was as impractical and unfeasible as netting a shark, a teacup containing the ocean, or holding the wind in one's hand.

Foolhardy and pointless.

And, in point of fact, someone was bound to get hurt.

Probably multiple someones.

After giving his precocious sister and his stepmother dutiful pecks upon their cheeks, Ronan shook Sanford's and Benjamin's hands.

As always, Sanford looked as if he'd swallowed a

whole sour pickle, and the vegetable had become wedged sideways in his throat. Or he'd overindulged in dates *again* and was suffering severe bowel cramps.

On the other hand, Benjamin, looking particularly dashing in a snug-fitting, claret-colored jacket and buff pantaloons, appeared as if he were on the brink of laughter.

Corrina observed them with eyes too wise and cynical for her two-and-twenty-years.

Ronan looked at each of his siblings in turn.

Why did he have the peculiar feeling they were assembled to present a united front with their parents for whatever this *matter* was?

With each passing moment, he became more convinced that whatever was afoot was no trivial issue.

"Well," he put forth when no one initiated the conversation. "What is so deuced urgent I was forced to leave my bed after a mere three hours sleep?"

He didn't bother to conceal his ungentlemanly gaping yawn. He was bloody exhausted to his marrow and didn't care who knew it.

Still, the unsettling silence prevailed for another fifteen *tick-tocks* of the mahogany longcase clock standing unobtrusively in the far corner, its brass face as expressionless as Pillington's.

Once again, Ronan interrupted the interminable quiet which hung like a heavy shroud in the room. "Couldn't whatever this problem is have waited until this afternoon when I'd rested a few hours?" he ventured, a trifle impatiently.

A problem so very crucial that his entire family except Marissa was assembled?

"No, it cannot," Sanford put in, all starchy somberness as was his wont. Not a raven hair out of place, his mahogany brown eyes brooding, he contemplated Ronan.

When was the last time he'd spontaneously smiled or laughed with unfettered joy?

Not since he'd been three or four years old, surely. Nay two.

How boring and dissatisfying it must be to take oneself so bloody seriously all of the time.

God help his future bride.

Ronan cocked a sardonic brow, knowing full well his elder brother would elucidate further but had simply paused for dramatic effect. Sanford had proven himself a brilliant speaker in Parliament because of his flair for theatrical intonations.

"It has already been delayed for several weeks as it is." Sanford gave their father a pointed look.

"*Weeks,* you say? As in more than one?" Ronan couldn't help but goad, earning him a steely stare from his elder brother.

The unspoken censure that Ronan had been in America instead of with his feet solidly planted on good ol' British soil might not have been verbalized but was apparent for all to hear.

His eldest brother disapproved of Ronan's

business ventures in the United States. Neither had he forgiven the "*bloody ungrateful, rebellious colonists*" for the War of 1812.

Sanford epitomized the traditional British aristocrat who believed the British superior in every way in everything. Such draconian thinking would eventually see the peerage destroyed. Only forward-thinking aristocrats would survive the changes asserting themselves upon the nobility, whether the upper ten thousand wanted to accept those changes or not.

Ronan gravitated his attention to his younger, much less pompous brother.

Grinning, Benjamin hooked his ankle over his knee and folded his arms rather smugly. Bobbing his Hessian-clad foot, he arched hawkish blond eyebrows in a failed attempt to appear innocent.

"I'm just here as a spectator," he said flippantly, darting his amused gaze to those present. He waved a hand, his grin growing impossibly more enormous still. "This is going to be jolly good fun."

"Hush, Benjamin. This is no laughing matter," their stepmother chided, eyeing Ronan with a somewhat unnerving contemplative maternal perusal. Rarely had she turned such speculative consideration on him.

Unease clawed Ronan's spine with its pointed little talons.

"Oh, Mama. Forgive me, but I quite disagree,"

Benjamin chuckled, wicked merriment glinting in his hazel eyes. "What say you, Corrina? *Is* this a laughing matter?"

As one, Ronan and his brothers looked to the elder of their sisters.

Corinna gave Ronan a probing glance with her incredible pale blue eyes before saying, "I think it shall prove quite…interesting." Head canted, she touched a fingertip to her chin. "I also believe you are all underestimating Ronan tremendously."

Well, one vote of confidence was better than none. And yet, Ronan still had no more idea why he'd been summoned than he had when he'd sleepily answered his door.

Rather peeved that he was the only person present who was ignorant of whatever the crucial matter was, he crossed to the ostentatious walnut desk. Barely suppressing a glower, he sank into the tufted burgundy wingback chair.

Still no coffee either.

Ronan's head was on the verge of exploding—as was his, up until this point, judiciously controlled temper.

Enough of this fustian prattle.

"Well?" Ronan snapped, tapping his fingers on the leather armrest. They made a faint cracking sound with each impatient tap.

Brow furrowed and uncharacteristically subdued, Father lifted two missives, the wax seals clearly broken on both. He extended the folded rectangles, one with black wax and the other a deep green.

"These are for you, Son."

Leaning forward, curiosity and a jot of trepidation pitching in his gut, Ronan accepted the letters. "You opened my correspondences?"

From his place behind the divan where their mother and Benjamin sat, Sanford said, "It was a matter of some urgency."

So everyone kept insisting, and yet Ronan still had no inkling what was afoot.

Arms clasped behind his back, Sanford reminded Ronan of a great crow, perched and ready to pounce. Posture rigid, a muscle flexed rhythmically in Sanford's jaw as he glanced out the window before leveling his gaze expectantly upon their father.

Could rigor mortis set in *before* a person died?

Ronan unfolded the first letter, but before he could read the salutation, Benjamin fairly crowed, "You, dear brother, have been named guardian to *two* young girls."

Mrs. Shepherd, I find myself in a most unique position. As you are vastly familiar with what happens to unwanted girls I seek your assistance. Sadly, my employer has departed this earth, and my two young charges' guardian has yet to contact us. Simply put, if I cannot make other arrangements for the Masterson girls, could you possibly find room at Haven House and Academy for the Enrichment of Young Women for them, though there isn't anyone to pay the usual fee? They've literally nowhere else to go.

~ Miss Mercy Feathers in a letter to Hester Shepherd Proprietress at Haven Home and Academy for the Enrichment of Young Women

5

Grosvenor Square, London
Marquess of Trentholm's manor
The next afternoon

R onan paced in his father's study as he awaited the solicitor, Joseph Bralen's, arrival. A sideways glance to the mahogany, inlaid longcase clock angled and patiently *tick-tocking* in the room's corner revealed the solicitor was twelve minutes late.

Guardian to Masterson's daughters?

The knowledge was surreal, and over four-and-twenty hours after Benjamin gleefully blindsided Ronan with the news, he still couldn't quite grasp the reality of the situation.

His family had judiciously decided the forthcoming meeting should only include the relevant parties: Ronan and the pesky solicitor.

Nonetheless, he was no addlepate. His father and Sanford—likely his other well-meaning but intrusive family members as well—would be upon him like cloying fog upon the Thames in wintertime the second Bralen set a foot onto the stoop afterward.

Releasing a lungful of air from between his clamped teeth—causing Ronan's lips to puff out in a childish fashion—he pointed what surely must be an agitated gaze ceilingward for a handful of steps.

He hadn't been this tense and apprehensive since the sinking of the *Nightingale.* Although this trepidation was of a wholly different sort. This time, his life wasn't in physical peril, but as surely as there was a God in heaven, his contented, comfortable, and highly enjoyable bachelor's existence was about to undergo a catastrophic change.

He cupped his nape to ease the knotted muscles there.

Mayhap not.

He might not have to give up his comfortable rooms and either move to his father's manor house—gargling glass shards was preferrable—or find a suitable townhome in London.

Or…could he simply leave the girls in their current residence and visit once or twice yearly?

Now, there was an idea worth pursuing.

Yes, that idea held real merit. Indeed, it did.

After all, many children, particularly progeny of the peerage, were left in the care of devoted servants.

Your parents will never permit it. Never.

An inconvenient but irrefutable truth there.

As unfashionable as it might be, the Trentholms were of the unpopular opinion that children thrived and were prone to far fewer temperamental or behavioral displays when their parents were frequently involved in their lives. Mother and Father would disapprove of Ronan shunting his soon-to-be wards off to a country estate to molder away.

He cringed at the less than appealing tableau that popped to mind at the thought.

His own blasted conscience seemed determined to thwart him at every turn.

What was more, Ronan still wanted to plant Benjamin a facer over his blatant delight that Ronan had been so put upon. In fact, should his smug brother show his face today, Benjamin would not depart Ronan's presence without him blackening his brother's eye.

How dare he openly gloat about Ronan's misfortune?

What a deuced, bloody inconvenience.

He'd planned to sail to America again in April or May at the latest.

Besides, what was he supposed to do with two girls?

What, pray tell, did he know of raising gently bred young women?

Nothing. Not a jot.

Mayhap Mother could be persuaded to lend her aid? Or...to take Masterson's daughters under her comforting wing and let— What were their names?

He paused to search the archives of his mind.

Bellamy and Arabelle.

Yes, that was right.

At least he remembered that much about them. If he'd been required to inform anyone their ages, beyond young, he'd have failed, however.

In any event, perchance, Mother *would* agree it was best for everyone to have Bellamy and Arabelle live with the marquess and marchioness. Constancy and stability. Two parental figures were better than a rapscallion bachelor.

Not that Ronan lived a licentious existence. Because he didn't.

Neither was he particularly pious.

True, he'd begged the Almighty to spare his life when the *Nightingale* sank and thanked the Lord profusely afterward as well. Yes, he attended services regularly when in London and even prayed every now and again. But he didn't consider himself a devout man.

Rubbing his nose, he shook his head.

Even as he pondered the possibility of his parents assuming responsibility for the Masterson girls, he knew full well that his optimism was misplaced.

Nay, the glint in his stepmother's eye yesterday did not suggest she would alleviate him of this new, wholly unwanted obligation.

There *might* be another recourse other than accepting the guardianship.

Would Masterson have appointed Ronan if there were?

No.

Not a leper's chance of an invitation to court, he wouldn't have done.

Lieutenant Masterson wasn't a man to leave anything to chance.

"Bloody d—," Ronan squelched the vulgar oath rising to his tongue.

As he turned to make the return trip across the Aubusson cranberry, juniper-green, and tobacco-brown carpet, his attention fell on the two letters stacked in the right corner atop Father's desk.

He'd perused both innumerable times and grudgingly admitted that his sire had been right to have read the missive from Bralen. Particularly as the solicitor had called at the marquess's residence no less than five times in the past several weeks in an effort to contact Ronan.

The man's dedication to his duties was

commendable, if somewhat annoying and perhaps even overbearing. Hadn't he repeatedly been told that he'd be notified the instant Ronan returned to England? At which time, the impending guardianship would be discussed down to the last maddening detail.

Did that Bralen fellow think calling every week would expedite the ship's voyage? Alter the ocean's currents? Impact the winds? Lessen the cargo hold's heavy load, which caused the vessel to ride low in the water?

In truth, Ronan mightn't have returned to England for another month or two or even more.

Guardianship.

A low growl slipped past his lips.

He'd truly been named a guardian, and to a pair of young females at that.

What in God's holy name did he know about such matters?

Again, something akin to dread burgeoned through him from his taut stomach to his constricted throat. At the forest-green, velvet festooned draperies, he pivoted and marched in the other direction again.

The second letter, only received a few days ago from a Miss Mercy Feathers, wasn't as official as Bralen's. Yet the missive could never be misconstrued as anything but an artfully crafted, professional correspondence.

Although Miss Feathers's letter was proper to the extreme, Ronan couldn't help but sense an undercurrent of disapproval woven into her perfectly articulated script.

Bralen's letter succinctly informed Ronan he'd been appointed guardian to Masterson's daughters and steward of their inheritance upon Lieutenant Lewis Masterson's demise on 7 January 1818.

However, Miss Feathers had politely inquired precisely *when* Ronan intended to meet his wards of *seven weeks and two days*—a definite jab there—and whether it would be prudent for her to search for a new governess position.

The latter was a definite not-as-long-as-he-drew-a-breath no.

At least Miss Feathers—

How long had she been governess to his wards—er, soon-to-be wards?

He speared a glance toward the letters once more.

Ah, yes.

She had been employed as their governess for five years.

At least Miss Feathers knew the Masterson girls well. And, of course, the girls would need a governess until he'd determined what to do with them. Someone they knew and were comfortable with was all the better. It would save him a tremendous amount of inconvenience and time. Not to mention alleviating distress for the children.

Plowing his fingers through his already mussed short hair, Ronan stopped at the window on the other side of the study that looked out upon the street. The dark, dreary, and blustery day kept all but the most intrepid inside. Even as he watched the few brave souls scuttling along the lane, a rickety hired hack rattled to a stop before the mansion.

The miserable, swayback nag pulling the equally saggy and worse-for-wear conveyance half-heartedly swished her tail in a defeated manner. The poor old creature ought to be inside a warm stable munching warm mash instead of plodding London's rain-slickened streets.

Carrying a walnut-colored leather satchel, a little stick of a man emerged from the vehicle. Even from this distance, Ronan could see the sharp angles of Bralen's skeletal cheek and jawbone. His functional black-caped cloak whipped around his stick-like calves as the solicitor held one bony hand to his hat. Squinting against the blustery wind, he peered up at the house.

Feeling like a child sneaking a peek at guests attending a glittering ball, Ronan edged into the draperies. Bralen was not at all the type of solicitor he'd expected Masterson to have retained, but appearances were oft' misleading.

That was one reason why Ronan generally gave everyone the benefit of the doubt and strove not to be judgmental. More than once, that philosophy had landed him in a spot of trouble.

For the truth of it was that appearances *could* and

often *did* say a great deal about a person. And while it was noble and benevolent to assume people were good and honest, many—a great many to be perfectly candid—were rotten and corrupt to their putrid cores.

A few moments later, Sturges rapped upon the doorframe of the open study door. "Joseph Bralen, Esquire, sir."

Standing before the fireplace, his hands clasped behind his back, Ronan lifted his attention from the frolicking flames.

"My lord." Sans his outerwear, Bralen gave a smart bow before his keen gaze raked over Ronan.

And found him wanting.

Ronan saw it in the faintest twitch of the man's upper lip and the disparaging, minutest narrowing of his eyes. And the way his attention had lingered on Ronan's less than artful cravat.

On the other hand, Mr. Bralen's neckcloth was a well-starched, simple but precise execution of folded and tied perfection.

In truth, Ronan didn't give a donkey's bray what the spindly solicitor thought of him.

"I beg your pardon for my tardiness. The roads were unusually congested for this time of day," Bralen said while taking in the room.

"It is of no matter, Mr. Bralen." Ronan swept his arm toward the desk. "Please. Have a seat."

After the slightest hesitation, the solicitor dipped his nearly bald head and marched toward the desk, his damp shoes squeaking with each step.

Squeak. Squelch. Squeak. Squelch.

Like a mouse. Or rat.

"The marquess will not be joining us?" Bralen asked, opening the clasps of his portfolio. He glanced up expectantly as Ronan took the chair behind his father's impressive desk.

"No. My father will not."

So, Ronan's assessment of Bralen's evaluation of him had been on the mark. The man thought him a rogue and a ne'er-do-well, incapable of making responsible decisions, much less assuming a guardianship.

Mr. Bralen cleared his throat, the sound like carriage wheels on frozen snow, and laid a thin, neat pile of documents upon the desk. In short order, he conveyed what Ronan already knew.

Masterson had died. He had no living relatives, and hence, he'd left the care of his daughters to Ronan. He'd also left his entire estate to his daughters.

Not that there was much to leave, as it turned out.

"As I've indicated, your lordship," Bralen said, his tone and mannerisms clipped and perfunctory, "the estate is mortgaged to such a great extent that the only viable option is to sell the house, lands, livestock, as well as other possessions and furnishings to pay Lieutenant Masterson's debts with the proceeds."

So much for leaving the girls in their current home.

"Even then, there won't be sufficient funds to fully cover the debts," Bralen said. "The lieutenant lived well beyond his means for some time."

Distinct disapproval hardened the lawyer's voice and shortened the syllables of the last sentence. Joseph Bralen, Esquire was a judgmental, condemning scunner. A pizzle in a waistcoat. A short, shriveled pizzle at that.

"Masterson was a naval hero who risked his life to save many men." Ronan leveled the solicitor a look that was meant to singe his grizzly eyebrows. "Were I you, Mr. Bralen, I would carefully consider further impugning the character of the man I owe my life."

Bralen's nervous gaze flicked to Ronan's scar.

Ronan gave a curt nod at the unspoken question.

He didn't owe this bugger any details, but if he besmirched Masterson's honor again...

The solicitor swallowed audibly, and his neckcloth wobbled as his Adam's apple skittered up and down his scrawny throat like a rodent trapped in linen.

Ronan pulled the documents toward him, indicating the matter was closed.

"I just thought you should be thoroughly apprised of the situation," Bralen mumbled, evidently too stupid to take a hint as broad as a ship.

An elbow resting on the desktop and two fingertips pressed to the bridge of his nose, Ronan swiftly read the documents. He gave no indication he'd heard the pesky solicitor whose gloom and doom attitude wore rather thin.

He'd do well with Sanford, however. They could bemoan the doleful fate of the world and its unworthy occupants together.

Ronan cursed beneath his breath as he flipped over another page.

Masterson had indeed been pockets to let. He'd kept that somber fact a well-guarded secret. Unwise investments after his wife's passing had contributed to the financial disaster he'd left behind.

Staring at the papers he'd just perused, Ronan sat back. What a bloody tangle. "I see how dire the circumstances are, Mr. Bralen. How have the servants' wages and the household expenses been paid since Masterson's death?"

He brought his gaze up to meet Bralen's.

Mouth opening and closing several times like a banked bass, Bralen blinked at Ronan. Finally, he croaked, "Sir?"

An uneasy feeling tingled along Ronan's spine. Lowering his hand, he tapped his fingers atop the documents. Anyone who knew him a jot knew that slight movement signaled exasperation.

He'd be bound, Masterson's servants had been working without pay these past seven weeks—*and two days*. Except it was closer to eight weeks now. Which also gave credence as to why Miss Feathers had taken it upon herself to write Ronan.

Did she resent being obligated to care for her

charges without compensation?

She *had* mentioned continued employment.

Ronan wasn't certain if that made her mercenary or judicious.

Naturally, he would see to hers and the other domestics' back wages.

"I assume you at least provided an allowance for food and other necessities," he said, mindful to keep his annoyance from his tenor. Few people were forthright if put on the defensive.

"No indeed, my lord. I would never have presumed to do so." Bralen drew himself up, his affront tangible. "That would've been beyond the scope of my authority."

As if Ronan had asked him to steal the Crown Jewels and pawn them to feed starving urchins.

"Besides, your lordship, there were no funds available. *None.* I expected the household had sufficient foodstuffs in reserve, and the staff was…are, that is…free to seek employment elsewhere."

The governess isn't, you bloody arse.

Ronan couldn't regret his lapse into vulgarity.

Who would've cared for his new wards had Miss Feathers taken it upon herself to abandon them?

Deep in Ronan's belly, molten anger stirred and sidled along his veins. A rare but dangerous thing.

This little rodent turd of a man hadn't bothered to ensure Masterson's daughters or his staff had provisions? Firewood? Coal? Bralen obviously knew nothing of the mechanisms of running a large household.

Wrestling his ire under control, Ronan modulated his tone and asked coolly, "How many servants did Lieutenant Masterson employ?"

Few people cared enough to worry about retainers when an estate was liquidated, as must happen in this case. The girls had not only lost their father, but they were going to lose their home as well, and likely the company of servants they'd known their entire lives.

Life was bloody, bloody unfair.

"Eight, including the...*governess*," Bralen said, a strange inflection entering his brusque tone. "Two recently left of their own volition. As for the others, I'm sure with letters of reference from the marquess..."

He trailed off at Ronan's steely glower.

Was Bralen even aware of how much of a condescending piece of excrement he was?

"Yes, well." The solicitor noisily cleared his throat. "With references, they shouldn't have any trouble finding new positions," Bralen muttered sourly. "Except for Miss Feathers, that is, your lordship."

"And why is that, Mr. Bralen? Why is Miss Feathers singularly undeserving of a recommendation?"

In Ronan's mind, a governess who stayed and cared for her charges without pay and who took it upon herself to write him inquiring about their futures was

58

deserving of admiration.

There is no finer person on earth, other than their governess, who I would trust Arabelle's and Bellamy's care to than you.

Masterson had obviously held the woman in high esteem. Regardless, he couldn't very well make her guardian of his daughters. It just wasn't done.

Bralen sniffed contemptuously.

"Her official capacity *might've* been that of a governess. However, I have reason to believe she played an *entirely* different role in Lieutenant Masterson's household."

The solicitor's meaning was as clear as one of the crystalline raindrops trailing down the study window. He might as well have called Mercy Feathers a slattern.

Ronan stiffened and drew his hand resting atop the desk into his lap, where he curled it into a tight fist. Teeth clamped, he barely restrained himself from springing from the chair, lunging across the desk, grabbing hold of Bralen's artful neckcloth, and shaking the man like a terrier with a rat.

Masterson had been devoted to his wife before her death. He hardly seemed the type to disrespect her memory and flagrantly flaunt a mistress in his house under the guise of a governess. Particularly at the risk of smudging his daughters' reputations.

His patience shredded, Ronan flexed his jaw and met Bralen's superior gaze directly.

"*What* precisely are you implying, Bralen?" The flinty look he leveled the solicitor had sent many a man to trembling in their footwear. "That Miss Feathers was Lieutenant Masterson's lady love?"

Instead of being cowed as any sensible man would've done, Bralen lifted his bulbous nose. The epitome of self-righteous superiority, he looked down its considerable length with an expression that was surely meant to intimidate but which only made him appear cross-eyed.

Ronan knew the solicitor's type well. Self-righteous, self-proclaimed saints, condemning and judging others while never noticing their own shortcomings or vices.

"Miss Feathers is far too attractive to be *just* a governess, my lord. No wife would have ever been foolish enough to have hired her. As I'm sure you know, men have *needs*. I am convinced that though she may have initially been retained to oversee the Masterson girls' education, Miss Feathers also…ah…erm…that is…warmed the lieutenant's bed."

At that mumbled, disparaging pronouncement, Bralen's ears burned a fiery reddish-purple.

If talking about sexual congress turned the man into a bumbling fool, he pitied the solicitor's wife.

Ronan leaned back into the chair, putting off an air of false serenity. Another trick he'd learned to put his adversaries at ease.

Was Joseph Bralen, Esquire an adversary?

Time would tell.

Originally, Ronan had intended to retain Miss Feathers as governess for the time being. However, if what Bralen alluded was true, that would be impossible. A woman of loose virtue would tarnish his wards' reputations.

"Have you any basis for your theory?" he asked casually, mindful of making Bralen believe they were of a like mind. "Any witnesses to her...ah...indiscretions or immoral behavior?"

Dirt-brown eyes glittering with cruel delight, Bralen nodded, looking very much like a trained parrot. "'Tis common knowledge in Rochester. Several people insinuated as much to me when I made inquiries about the extent of the lieutenant's debt. Also," he went on, his scrawny chest swelling in self-satisfaction, "when I advised the merchants to extend no further credit in Lieutenant Masterson's name."

What in hellfire?

Not only had this maggot not provided monies for Masterson's household to live on, but he'd also severed all lines of credit too.

How had they managed?

Perhaps desperation had prompted Miss Feathers's bold correspondence.

Guilt tightened the wad in Ronan's stomach. Though why he should feel guilty when he hadn't even been aware of Masterson's passing made no sense.

"*That,* Mr. Bralen, is gossip. I do not base decisions or actions on rumors or tattle. Have you anyone, a single person, who can vouch with absolute confidence that Miss Feathers was Lieutenant Masterson's mistress?"

The solicitor gave an eager nod again as he withdrew another document and slid it across the desk to Ronan.

Ronan glanced down, and his stomach constricted impossibly more.

The deuced guardianship contract.

"Yes, indeed, my lord," Bralen, all but crowed. "A former maid, Cammie Sumner, vowed she'd seen Miss Feathers leaving the lieutenant's bedchamber on multiple occasions."

You are right to be concerned on Mercy's behalf,
Purity. Please keep our dear friend in your prayers.
Doctor Morrisette told me just yesterday afternoon
that he has heard ugly whispers in Rochester about
Mercy. Brandon says his patients babble on about all
Manner of things, and many of them love nothing
better than to share the latest on dit. They claim
Mercy was the lieutenant's mistress. Of course, we
know how utterly ludicrous such an accusation
is. Regardless, if this defaming slander
spreads, she might not be able to find
a new position. I must warn her.

~ Mrs. Joy Morrisette in a letter to
Miss Purity Mayfield

6

Rochester, England
Masterson residence
4 March 1818
Midmorning

Hands on her hips, Mercy perused the salon she'd just tidied. Another task she'd taken on since the last maid had left five days ago. That same day, Mercy had tossed the only remaining bouquet of wilted lilies in the rubbish bin. If she never saw another lily for as long as she lived and breathed, she would not regret it.

Today, the salon's tall windows stood wide open, letting in the fresh spring air.

It was still quite chilly outside. However, last week, the rain had, at last, ceased soaking the earth, and the ground had finally dried out. The verdant tips of a few intrepid daffodils bravely peeked above the rich, dark soil visible just beyond the open windows.

The world went on as if nothing had changed.

Everything had changed.

Since she'd posted her letter to Ronan Brockman, almost another fortnight had passed without a word from him or Mr. Bralen.

Inconsiderate blackguards.

With each passing day, Mercy's apprehension, and yes, her anger and frustration, grew.

Three more servants had left after finding new positions. Only Mrs. Stanley, the aging cook, and Norman, the gardener and sometimes stable hand, had remained. Both were too advanced in years to contemplate willingly leaving or easily finding new employment.

Honestly, Mercy wasn't surprised at the other domestics' departures. Her funds were depleted—gone, in truth—and the mysterious guardian remained ominously and conspicuously absent.

She pointed her gaze to the floor for a few heartbeats, willing the surge of unease billowing in her middle to abate. The truth of it was that she'd exhausted her savings—her only protection and buffer against an inhospitable future.

Could she even acquire a new position without a letter of reference?

Regardless, she didn't—*couldn't*—regret her impoverishment or the cause thereof. Nevertheless, that didn't lessen the trepidation that had become a constant, lurking companion. As unwelcome as mildew and equally as challenging to be rid of.

Though Mercy had economized in every conceivable way, the funds had dwindled from a windmill to a nutshell in short order. A governess's wages were never meant to sustain a household or stables the size of Masterson's.

How could she have done otherwise though?

Her very first memories at Haven House and Academy for the Enrichment of Young Women included gentle admonitions about sharing and selflessness—charity and assisting those in need. And for certain, Arabelle and Bellamy were in need, even if they were blissfully unaware of that nasty fact.

Last night, as Mercy had lain awake in her bed again—a much too common occurrence since the lieutenant's death—she'd made a bold, perhaps not entirely wise or logical decision.

Keep on being courageous and strong.

Be courageous and He will strengthen your heart.

Shoulders squared, she gave a small, determined nod.

She would take Arabelle and Bellamy to London. To that prestigious Grosvenor Square address she'd found listed for Mr. Negligent, Self-Centered, Uncaring, Beastly Lord Ronan Brockman. She knew only the poshest, wealthiest members of *le beau monde* resided in Mayfair.

Arabelle and Bellamy would not go hungry under her watch, by George.

Besides, Mercy saw no other alternatives.

Unless…

She eyed the vases on the rosewood tables and then the gewgaws situated around the room on various shelves and surfaces.

Did she dare sell any of them?

Or the four horses and two ponies in the stables?

Would it constitute theft if she did—even if it was to purchase necessities for the girls?

Mercy Augusta Judith Shepard Feathers, stealing is a sin.

Yes. Yes, of course, it was. Mercy's conscience upbraided her for even considering such a deplorable thing for an instant.

Arabelle and Bellamy owned everything now. Children were hardly capable of giving their governess permission to sell their possessions so they might have food on the table. The dears had no idea how very dire their circumstances were.

Mercy intended they remain oblivious. Such matters were the worry and responsibility of adults, not innocent children.

She'd promised the girls a grand adventure this morning when she'd explained they'd journey to London on the morrow. Even now, Bellamy and Arabelle were in the nursery deciding which dolls must accompany them.

They were permitted one, and only one, each. As it was, the mail coach mightn't have enough room for all of their bags and Fluffer-Muffer's basket.

Before Mercy could pack herself, she must take the pony cart to the other side of Rochester and pawn her silver cross brooch, a parting gift from Hester Shepherd. It was Mercy's most treasured possession and only piece of jewelry.

Pressing a palm to her forehead, she swallowed against the familiar sting of tears.

Setting her jaw, she blinked away the moisture.

This wasn't the time for self-pity. She hadn't let herself contemplate what Brockman's lack of response meant. The uncertainty gnawed at her innards to such an extent she found it impossible to eat. Which was just as well as it meant more food for the others.

She'd lost weight, and she'd been slender to begin with.

Fifteen minutes later, Mercy tied the ebony ribbons of her unadorned black bonnet beneath her chin. After checking on Bellamy and Arabelle, who'd been assigned the task of finding where Fluffer-Muffer had hidden herself today, and with a gentle but firm warning to the girls not to be a trial to Mrs. Stanley, she addressed the cook.

"I shouldn't be away longer than an hour or so, I don't imagine, Mrs. Stanley," Mercy said. "I've told the girls to come to the kitchens straightaway after finding Fluffer-Muffer. I'll wager the cat's in the lieutenant's bedchamber again. I suppose I ought to lock the door, but I know Arabelle and Bellamy still like to spend time in there."

After all, Lieutenant Masterson's chamber with his brushes, shaving kit, and clothing were the last vestiges they had of their father. They often forgot to close the door when they left, and inevitably, Fluffer-Muffer found her way inside to curl up on his bed.

Had she not witnessed the phenomenon herself, Mercy wouldn't have believed an animal capable of mourning as much as Fluffer-Muffer had.

The cook glanced up from the onion she'd been chopping for tonight's watery soup and nodded. "I'll prepare the little mites a spot of tea, and they can enjoy a slice of warm bread with it."

Neither mentioned the lack of butter or preserves to top the golden-crusted loaves cooling on a long table beneath a wide window. At least they still had flour for bread—not much, however.

Giving in to an impulse, Mercy hugged the shorter, much rounder woman. Even Mrs. Stanley's gown hung slightly looser on her, a testament to her sacrifice as well.

"Thank you, Mrs. Stanley."

Blushing, the cook tucked her chin to her chest, *tsking* under her breath with embarrassment. "Get on with you now, miss. I cannot be responsible for your charges all afternoon."

Cook adored the girls and welcomed their company. She'd become teary-eyed when Mercy had confessed her intention to journey to London tomorrow.

"I'll hurry back from town. I promise," Mercy assured her. "I cannot imagine I'll be above a couple of hours."

For the umpteenth time, she pressed her fingers to the reticule hanging from her wrist, checking to ensure the silver brooch was inside. Striding to the entrance, she tried to calculate how much the piece of jewelry might be worth.

Lord, let it be enough, and please don't let me be swindled.

As Mercy hurried along the corridor, the front knocker echoed forcefully.

Oh, no.

She stopped midstride, unease scuttling across her shoulders.

Another merchant collecting an outstanding debt?

There'd been a steady stream of men banging upon the front door the past ten days. They'd permitted a respectable passage of time after the lieutenant's death, but their patience had come to an end, and now the creditors and moneylenders wanted their coin.

How could her deceased employer have owed so many people so much?

More on point, how had he kept his financial woes hidden?

He'd never been a day late with her wages or the other servants' either, to her knowledge. Which meant he must've had an income source of some sort. She, however, had no idea what that might've been.

Of late, she'd taken to perusing the daily post's return addresses to see if anything caught her eye before she added the unopened correspondences to the growing stack atop Lieutenant Masterson's desk.

She presumed the new guardian would deal with such matters. For although she'd essentially taken on the role of housekeeper, amongst other things, she couldn't impose and read someone else's communications. To do so would be beyond the pale.

It seemed too intrusive. Too personal. Too great an invasion.

The brass lion's head knocker resounded again. So caught up in her reveries, Mercy actually jumped at the jarring impact.

Botheration.

Whomever he was, he apparently wasn't going away.

At this moment, she didn't particularly consider persistence a virtue.

Mercy cast a longing glance in the direction she'd just come. She could escape out the kitchen or one of the other doors and let Mrs. Stanley answer.

But she wouldn't.

Mercy was not a coward.

Squaring her shoulders and stiffening her spine, Mercy marched forward. She'd just tell whoever this person was the same thing she'd told all of the others. They'd have to await the convenience of the girls' remiss guardian to have their delinquent accounts settled.

If Lord Ronan Brockman settled them.

Regardless, some merchants were becoming quite agitated in their demands. Mercy didn't blame them, but what did they expect her to do? They must be aware she didn't have access to Lieutenant Masterson's funds.

Mr. Emile Ryerson, the owner of Ryerson's Tailoring and Haberdashery, was beyond crotchety when he called yesterday. He'd declared that if Lieutenant Masterson's outstanding bill wasn't paid forthright, he would pursue legal alternatives. In fact, he declared he would contact the magistrate and demand the official confiscate property in lieu of the amount owed.

Then the philanderer had suggested a lewd and wholly abhorrent way in which Mercy might cancel a portion of the outstanding debt.

It wasn't *her* debt, as he well knew, yet the tosspot had attempted extortion.

She might've brandished a fire poker aimed at an

especially tender area of Mr. Ryerson's anatomy as he rapidly and wisely opted to depart the premises.

That had been another reason Mercy had concluded she had no choice but to go in search of Lord Ronan Brockman. The merchants and creditors expected payments she could not make, and after Mr. Ryerson's disgusting proposition, she worried about her own safety.

In truth, she had no idea why Joseph Bralen, Esquire had not settled those outstanding debts as yet. Her already less than flattering opinion of the solicitor had sunk even lower.

Somewhere above maggots and grubs but lower than vermin.

If the illustrious nobleman she was going to London in search of refused to do what was right, she would take Bellamy and Arabelle with her to Haven House and Academy for the Enrichment of Young Women.

Mrs. Shepherd would not turn them away.

Of that, Mercy was fairly confident.

Nonetheless, Mrs. Shepherd would expect Mercy to swiftly find employment, which left the question of what to do with the Masterson sisters when she did?

Haven House and Academy for the Enrichment of Young Women was not a charitable establishment. Anonymous sources paid exorbitant fees for each girl ensconced there. Castoffs and by-blows secreted a way to hide someone's disgrace.

Knock. Knock.

Knock-knock-knock-knock.

KNOCK.

Agitated and her temper simmering, Mercy yanked the door open amid the last impatient crack of brass upon brass.

"May I help you?" she asked a trifle more vehemently and less graciously than was her wont.

She had no time to dawdle if she were to pawn the brooch, purchase tickets on the mail coach, and return and pack for tomorrow's predawn departure.

An impossibly tall gentleman wearing a navy-blue triple caped greatcoat and an Oxonian hat stared down at her. A smile fashioned to liquify steel quirked up one side of his mouth in a sun-browned face.

She followed the narrow, buckled flesh lashing from his ear to his striking jaw and lower with her gaze. The scar should've detracted from his good looks, but in a peculiar way, the blemish enhanced his attractiveness. One side of his face was aristocratic perfection and the other marred by puckered flesh.

Above all, he exuded effortless elegance.

A crestless gleaming black coach and four stood in the circular drive, and she puzzled her brow.

Who was he?

He hadn't answered her initial query, and so, tilting her head back, she met his glittering brown gaze brimming with undisguised merriment.

The feeling of having slipped into a pool of warm,

sweet chocolate engulfed her.

Good Lord.

Irrationally affected by this stranger, Mercy cleared her throat. Probably just another debt collector, albeit an unusually young and attractive one.

Not that she was making a mental note of his features.

Well-bred ladies of questionable origins were not permitted such luxuries.

He wasn't from Rochester, she was reasonably confident. She stifled the groan which threatened. That could only mean news of Lieutenant Masterson's death had spread, and he owed additional debts.

Well, this handsome chap with his fancy coach would have to wait—just like all of the others.

"If you're here to collect a debt of Lieutenant Masterson, you have wasted your time. You'll have to take the matter up with either his solicitor, Joseph Bralen, Esquire, or the estate's newly appointed guardian, Lord Ronan Brockman."

She was quite proud she'd managed to modulate her tone and to hide her disdain of his lordship. Perchance using the guardian's honorific would intimidate this dashing fellow a little, and he'd quietly take his leave.

Or not.

Several awkward seconds passed, and with each, her tension grew at the delay of her departure. Only a crow's harsh cawing in the distance interrupted the weighty silence.

He continued to gaze at her with a hint of amusement in his warm eyes and crooked, sideways smile. And he still hadn't uttered a syllable.

Mayhap he was a bit off in the head.

Not a debt collector but perhaps lost?

It mattered not. Mercy needed to be on her way at once. She'd leave through the kitchen instead.

"I bid you a good day." With a crisp nod, she made to shut the door, but he had the audacity to shove his booted foot in the gap.

Why the rude...

Mercy mentally searched for a word that wouldn't make Mrs. Shepherd cringe and which wouldn't offend the Almighty. She settled on pinhead—most disappointing and inadequate for her current vexation.

Rude, codpate pinhead.

Well, that assuredly wasn't nearly as satisfactory as fat-headed arse or brazen bloody bugger.

A hot flush stole up her neck for even thinking such spiteful and offensive thoughts.

"You are going out?" the stranger inquired in a honey-smooth, slightly husky tone that nearly unhinged her knees.

Arching a starchy brow, she bent her mouth into a sardonic half-smile.

"Ah, you're a sharp one, you are," she said with exaggerated deference. She leaned in a few inches and almost jerked backward at the impact of his manly scent: sandalwood, starch, and a hint of something woodsy.

75

Recovering, she quipped, "What gave away my intentions? My bonnet, or was it my cloak?"

The words spilled from her lips before she was even aware. Aghast at her impudence and insolence, she caught the inside of her cheek between her teeth. She'd been unpardonably unkind to a man she suspected might have more hair than wit.

Good heavens.

What had come over her?

A slight frown wrinkling his forehead, the stranger took in her plain bonnet and slate gray cloak. The cloak truly ought to have been black to adhere to mourning protocol, but she wasn't spending money on a new one.

Mercy bristled anew at his bold perusal.

Who was this man that he should be so presumptuous?

More on point and of greater concern was, why was she responding with such rancor?

"Where are you going?" he queried, that formerly constrained jollity in his gaze giving into full-blown merriment at her disapproving scowl.

Why, the bounder was baiting her. Poking the tiger.

"That, sir, is none of your business," she said in her most professional governess's tone. The one she rarely had to use to chastise Arabelle or Bellamy for a social infraction. She was somewhat out of practice at being stern and commanding.

He grinned then, a full-mouthed flash of pure masculinity.

Mother of God.

Was her jaw sagging?

Her eyes bugging from their sockets?

Because her pulse was doing something quite irregular, as were her lungs. The dratted organs appeared to have forgotten how to inhale and exhale without conscious thought on her part.

Although she'd been raised as a pious young woman, Mercy felt something wholly *unholy* spring to life in her middle.

"Oh, I believe it is very much my business, Miss Mercy Feathers."

He knew her name.

That fact slashed through her unchaste musings, and her jaw went slack.

Oh, no, no, no.

Still with his foot wedged in the doorway, he swept his hat off, revealing rich brown hair much too luxurious and silky to be a man's. He bent into a brief but elegant bow.

She knew who he was before his name passed his firm lips.

Lord Ronan Brockman.

"Lord Ronan Brockman at your service."

A noise somewhere between a groan and a whimper escaped her parted lips.

She felt the hectic blush flaring across her face and racing up to singe the roots of her hair as his words registered.

Bother and rot.

It really is the most intriguing thing, Cathryn. My middle brother, the world traveler, free-spirited roué, named a guardian. And mind you, his wards are not little boys, which I believe he would be quite adequate at supervising. No, indeed. Ronan's charges are young girls. I shall keep you abreast of all the details. The Masterson sisters arrive within a fortnight. I think Ronan shall surprise us all, however—most of all himself.

~ Miss Corrina Brockman in a letter to
Miss Cathryn Knighton

Masterson residence
Twenty very long minutes later

Having been relieved of his greatcoat, gloves, and hat by Miss Feathers, Ronan paced Lieutenant Masterson's comfortable salon as he awaited the arrival of his charges and an overdue introduction. The tasteful furnishings were homey and welcoming, though no fire burned in the hearth as the chilly day would seem to require.

Likely, the tastefully decorated salon was only used for company, and as Miss Feathers hadn't expected anyone today, no fire had been lit. He could appreciate the wisdom of economizing but couldn't help but wonder if the rest of the house was as drafty and cold.

A shame the place was already on the market.

Though the estate lacked the majestic rolling lawns and grand sweeping drive of Kelvingrove Park—the marquessate's country seat—it truly was a charming home in a bubonic fashion.

Ronan couldn't quite stifle the guilt that poked him at his decision to sell Masterson's property. He had authorized Mr. Bralen to discreetly put the place on the market that afternoon they'd met in the Marquess of Trentholm's study.

He had the unpleasant task of informing his new wards and their governess of that unfortunate situation. This house was their home no longer, which they might've expected temporarily. However, he felt quite certain that no one, other than Mr. Bralen and perhaps Masterson himself, had considered they would never walk these halls again.

For all of ten irrational seconds, Ronan had pondered purchasing the property himself but had discarded the notion just as speedily. It was one thing to visit his wards at their home when they were the beneficiaries of said property. It was another thing entirely to acquire the mansion and then try to explain to Masterson's daughters why it was no longer theirs.

It was much too complicated, and in the long run,

Ronan feared it might've led to thorny relationships. Better, in this case, for the girls to start anew in London surrounded by his family. Father had a lovely country seat and multiple other mansions scattered around England. Mayhap one of those would become Bellamy and Arabelle's permanent residence.

Which meant Ronan would be under his father's thumb all the more.

A coarse sailor's curse tickled the back of his teeth, but he restrained himself and instead muttered "Sweet Jesus" beneath his breath.

Unlike his brothers, he wanted to make his own way in the world. He didn't want the fact that his father was a powerful lord to pave the way for opportunities or favors. Ronan far preferred to forge his own convoluted path, even if that meant he made mistakes. So far, his judgment and investments had proved sound, and he'd amassed a small but respectable fortune.

Although Ronan had intended to set out for Rochester straightaway after meeting with Joseph Bralen, the marquess, of course, had much different plans. Plans which included preparations for Masterson's daughters' arrival in Mayfair. Therefore, Ronan would also move back into the Trentholm mansion, set back from the street and conveniently— *or most inconveniently*—possessing several unoccupied bedchambers.

Neither of his parents would hear of him letting a

house in London to accommodate his new wards when there were well-appointed bedchambers, a nursery, and a schoolroom sitting empty in the ostentatious manor. Nor would they conceive, as he'd already deduced, that the girls should take up residence in Mayfair while he retained his comfortable bachelor's rooms.

That desperate dream had been the stuff of which fantasies were spun.

Of all the things Ronan had envisioned after learning Masterson had appointed him guardian to his daughters, taking up residence under the Marquess of Trentholm's roof once again had not topped the list as desirable options.

In fact, it wasn't on any list. Ronan had never expected to reside under his father's roof again except for an occasional visit.

Nonetheless, he'd finally conceded to the logic of such an arrangement. Once the necessary details had been attended to and his belongings had been delivered to his former bedchamber, a peculiar sense of peace had settled inside him.

This was the right thing to do—the best thing for Arabelle and Bellamy.

For now, at least.

Ronan was no chucklehead. He readily acknowledged that he required his mother and sisters' help in this endeavor. What he knew about raising little girls wouldn't fill a salt spoon.

The image of Miss Mercy Feathers's expression

when he'd addressed her by her name and then introduced himself brought another round of chuckles. A concert of emotions had played across the delicate angles of her face: incredulity, shock, mortification, resignation, and finally, obsequiousness.

Why the latter peeved him, he couldn't identify. He far preferred the spirited woman who'd yanked the door open and told him to be on his way than the deferential servant who'd led him to the salon.

Bralen had mentioned the governess was pretty.

He'd grossly understated the truth.

Mercy Feathers was, in a word, exquisite.

She'd quite literally stolen his breath. For several excruciating heartbeats in which the organ had thrashed around behind his breast bone, he couldn't draw a single breath or blink.

Possessed of green eyes the shade of the lush woodland ferns he'd seen in America and the most striking red-gold hair he'd ever laid eyes upon, had she debuted for a London Season, she'd have been an original.

A diamond of the first water, assuredly. The incomparable of the Season.

Alabaster skin, so creamy and smooth as to be almost ethereal, had flushed a pretty peony pink when she'd realized who he was. Her bronze-tipped eyelashes had fluttered closed for a heartbeat, creating a thick fringe of lush mahogany fans on her flawless cheeks.

With commendable resolve, Miss Feathers had gathered her scattered composure and invited him inside.

"I beg your pardon, my lord," she'd said, the dual ribbons of her peach-tinted lips thinning the merest bit. "Do come in."

Nothing in her bearing, comportment, or attire suggested she was a flirt, demimonde, or in any way the immoral seductress Bralen had implied.

"*Her* sort is never content with being subservient," Bralen had said, contempt sharpening the edges of his derision. "They'll use their body and wiles to seduce a Godly man. The Bible warns us of sirens like Miss Feathers. Best be on your guard, my lord. She'll not be happy when she receives her *congé*. I'd advise you to not give her a letter of reference either. She'll just prey on another poor unsuspecting soul. He'll soon become besotted, and she'll entangle him in her web of sin."

The solicitor had peered so hard at Ronan during that last part that he hadn't a doubt the man directed his unkind speculations at him.

Web of sin, indeed.

Ronan would warrant that the only person spinning tales was the intolerant solicitor.

"When I require *your* advice, Mr. Bralen, I shall ask for it," Ronan had replied.

By that point, the arctic air was far warmer than either his tenor or demeanor.

As if he'd ever take up with a woman in his employ.

The Brockman men did not dally with their female staff, and neither did the current marquess or his father before him.

"A true gentleman never forces his attentions on a female in his employ. She won't resist your overtures because respectful positions are precious commodities for women. Remember that, my boys," Father had said. "Treat your female employees with the same respect you'd want your mother and sisters treated should, God forbid, their circumstances ever be reduced."

Hands clasped behind his back, Ronan perused the tidy, tastefully decorated room. Not the garish display of wealth he so often observed amongst *le beau monde*, but quality, comfortable furnishings meant to be used.

The staff was diligent, despite their master having passed just over two months ago. Their devotion was commendable as well. Few servants stayed on without wages for that long. He would promptly set to rights that oversight and include a much-deserved bonus for the staff's loyalty.

He hadn't yet decided what to do about Miss Mercy Feathers.

Take her to London or dismiss her?

Running a finger down his scar, he stared out the window at the gardens showing the first brave signs of spring.

He'd not pass judgment based on another's

accusations—especially Bralen's. The man was a sycophant toad. Something about him made Ronan's spine tingle in wariness. Besides, dismissing Miss Feathers might prove catastrophic regarding his new wards.

She knew them.

He didn't.

It was as simple as that.

Bellamy and Arabelle must be at the forefront of all of Ronan's considerations forthwith—including when he would next sail to India or America.

Mayhap he'd need to postpone his next journey.

Soft murmurings and the sounds of small feet approaching alerted him to his wards' arrival. Striving to don an inviting mien, he faced the doorway, angling his profile so that the girls would first see the unblemished side of his face.

Experience had taught him that his scar could be off-putting for those unprepared for the sight. Toward that end, he'd requested Miss Feathers alert Arabelle and Bellamy to his arrival and his disfigurement.

She'd skimmed her keen gaze over his scar, and he detected no revulsion. Neither had she averted her attention as many women did upon first seeing the ravaged flesh.

"As you wish, my lord. I shall advise them. But your scar isn't disfiguring," she'd said matter of factly. "You should know that the girls are not shallow creatures who judge others based on appearances.

They are kindhearted and considerate young ladies and understand that character is far more important than someone's looks."

Ronan would be bound that was because of their governess's instruction.

Holding a little dark-haired, doe-eyed girl by either hand, Miss Feathers advanced a couple of feet into the room. A rather large, long-haired gray cat with the brightest green eyes he'd ever seen meandered in behind them.

It stopped short upon spying Ronan. To his astonishment, the cat padded directly to him and, making little chirping noises, rubbed its head against his boots.

Ronan bent and scratched behind the friendly cat's ears. "Well, hello."

"She likes him," whispered one of the girls in wonderment.

"She always liked Papa best too," came the other child's soft reply.

"Fluffer-Muffer," Miss Feathers admonished, her cheeks slightly flushed. "Leave his lordship alone. Go lie down."

In all of his years, Ronan had yet to witness a single cat ever obeying its owner's directive. This one planted her ample haunches on the floor beside his boot and gave Miss Feathers a rather torpid stare which seemed to say, "Make me."

"Fluffer-Muffer?" he couldn't help but ask as he

stood upright once more.

The smallest Masterson girl nodded shyly. "Yes, because I wanted to name her Fluffy, and Bellamy wanted to name her Muffin." She lifted her shoulders and made a wry face. "So Miss Mercy suggested a comp...comp..." She glanced upward at her governess. "What is that word?"

"Compromise, dear," Miss Feathers replied with an affectionate smile and sweep of her hand across Arabelle's head.

"Yes, a compro-mise," the little girl echoed.

"Fluffer-Muffer," Miss Feathers repeated, extending her index finger to a nearby chair. "Go lie down."

After giving Miss Feathers a dismissive glance, silvery tail high in the air, the creature pranced to the armchair. She jumped onto the cushion with the intrinsic grace cats possess and, with another disdainful hooded gaze, proceeded to groom herself.

An obedient cat. It seems there *was* a first for everything.

A half-grin pulling at the corners of his mouth, Ronan shifted his attention back to his wards. Masterson's daughters had their father's eye and hair color, and there was a familiar angle to their chins.

That, however, was where the resemblance ended.

Ronan directed his regard to the smiling, tranquil woman in pink in the portrait above the fireplace. Yes, his wards took after their mother in every other respect.

An undefinable sensation prickled behind his ribs—an impulse to protect these three vulnerable females who were at his mercy and the harsh world's too. How much trust they were being forced to impart on him, and that reality humbled Ronan in a way nothing before ever had.

It also scared the bloody spit out of him.

*What you ask is simply not possible, my dear.
I wish it were otherwise, but I am sure you
understand the many reasons why it simply
wouldn't do. I only take on anonymous infants
at Haven House and Academy for the Enrichment
of Young Women. I am granted the sole right of
guardianship for those unwanted waifs. Should
word get out that Haven House has become a refuge
for any young girl in dire straits, I could no longer
cater to the exclusive clientele I serve. You must use
all of your skills to ensure the girls' new guardian
accepts the position. I am confident you will do so.
After all, you were one of my best students.*

~ Mrs. Hester Shepherd in a letter to
Miss Mercy Feathers

8

*Masterson residence
The salon*

Before Ronan could wrap his mind around that
truth, Miss Feathers cleared her throat.

Halfway into the room, with a gentle palm to
either of their narrow shoulders, she guided the girls
forward. Each wore black from toe to top, as was the
custom for those in mourning. Nevertheless, it only

served to remind Ronan how much these three females had lost.

How very dependent they were, including Miss Feathers, on others' munificence.

It was a precarious position at best, more so for the governess. At this juncture, she did not have a letter of reference, and Ronan still hadn't decided what course to take with her. The truth of it was—and it was very unlike him to waffle about important decisions—he rather thought how she presented herself the next few days would decide the matter.

That and the glaring issue as to whether she'd been Masterson's mistress.

He swept his gaze over her, aiming for impartial scrutiny and failing miserably.

In short, Miss Mercy Feathers was an extremely desirable woman, even draped in understated mourning togs and her hair swept into a tight chignon. Nothing about her gown was the least provocative, and yet…yet there was an unmistakable aura of femininity about her.

That allure had beckoned to him from the instant she'd thrown the front door open and demanded to know what he wanted.

Ronan hadn't decided whether it was a deliberate ploy on the governess's part or if it was an intrinsic part of Miss Feathers's nature. Some women emanated a miasma of seduction. When they learned to use that gift to mesmerize men… Well, the mythical sirens who lured sailors to their deaths were amateurs compared to those Jezebels.

The question was, was Miss Feathers one of them?

Dragging his attention from the woman who'd plagued his thoughts far more than he'd care to admit, Ronan examined Bellamy and Arabelle.

The black frocks gave his wards a washed-out complexion, but the somber shade on Miss Feathers only accented her glorious strawberry blond hair, ivory skin, peach-tinted lips, and stunning green eyes.

Enough.

He ordered his male appreciation to stow it.

Only a complete debaucher and libertine looked upon his employees with anything other than a professional eye. And for the immediate future, Miss Feathers was in his employ.

Other than slightly pale, Ronan's charges looked well. Their eyes were bright, their clothing well-tended, and their hair neatly brushed and plaited. They were slight of frame, but that wasn't unusual for growing children.

Unless...had they gone hungry these past months?

From beneath hooded eyelids, he examined Miss Feathers more closely. Her gown hung slightly loose on her willowy frame, and a frown pulled his eyebrows together. Had grief for her lover dampened her appetite, or had lack of food caused her weight loss?

Summoning what he hoped was a warm, paternal smile, Ronan half bowed. "I am very pleased to finally have the pleasure of meeting you, Miss Bellamy and Miss Arabelle. I regret I didn't come sooner. I was in America on business and only just returned."

The corners of Miss Feathers' eyes flexed the merest bit.

What? Had she thought him negligent on purpose?

"Your father was a great friend of mine," Ronan said with an easy smile meant to put the girls at ease. "In fact, he saved my life."

Miss Feathers's attention veered to his scar for a fraction before flitting away.

Astute woman. She'd made the connection without him having to explain how he'd come by his injury.

At his admission that Masterson had been Ronan's friend, a bit of the girls' wariness eased. They cast cautious glances at Miss Feathers before slowly stepping forward. Each executed a perfect curtsy while simultaneously saying, "My lord."

"Oh, none of that 'my lord' business, please." Grinning, he winked. "My father, the marquess, is *my lord*, and my eldest brother quite likes all that pomposity. Sanford most assuredly would expect you to address him as *my lord*. However, I would consider it the highest honor if you were to call me Ronan as my friends do. For, I do hope we shall be friends."

Sanford wouldn't approve. But then again, Ronan's older brother didn't approve of most things.

The girls exchanged wary, uncertain glances, then

sent questioning looks to their governess, seeking her approval.

To be perfectly proper, as he was a marquess's second son, his wards ought to address him as Brockman until they became better acquainted. He could almost see the wheels in Miss Feathers's pretty head churning away as she tried to decide what would be appropriate.

Or…did she think he tested her on her knowledge of etiquette?

Were there hard and fast rules for how one's wards addressed their guardian?

Likely there were, but he had no idea what those strictures might be, and neither of his parents had thought to impart to him any wisdom they might have on the matter. Sanford would likely have a stack of fusty books on the subject, probably memorized word for word, while Ronan's youngest three siblings would agree with him.

Using given names always lent to a closer relationship.

"Perhaps Lord Ronan for the present?" Miss Feathers said in that rich, dulcet tone that made him feel as if he'd slipped into a hot bath liberally dosed with almond oil.

Very clever.

Just inside the boundaries of respectability.

"Yes, that's perfectly fine," Ronan agreed reassuringly. "Whatever you young ladies are the most comfortable with."

He included the pretty governess in the invitation. Her green eyes rounded a trifle before she reshaped her features into a placid mask of subservience.

Ronan far preferred the spitfire who greeted him at the door and tried to shut the panel in his face. He'd also wager she hadn't acted the docile servant for Masterson.

Her eyes still flashed with some unspoken emotion.

There was something familiar about Miss Feathers, and he wracked his brain trying to pinpoint just what it was. It was her eyes, he finally decided. He vowed he'd met someone with eyes very much like hers and that pert nose that crinkled in a rather charming fashion when she was vexed.

However, that was neither here nor there.

Arms folded, Ronan assessed his wards. They appeared healthy and obviously trusted their governess. They'd edged back to her side, and Miss Feathers had slipped an arm about their waists, cocooning them protectively.

That she was genuinely fond of them was also apparent.

Excellent.

She had been the nurturing female in their household for most of the girls' lives, and their bond was unmistakable.

There is no finer person on earth, other than their governess.

That line from Masterson's letter to Ronan marched across his mind.

Because Miss Mercy Feathers was a genuinely exceptional governess or because Masterson's relationship with her was something more than professional?

Setting aside that dilemma for now, Ronan angled his chin toward the taller of the girls. "I presume you are Bellamy?"

Expression somber, Bellamy nodded once, then directed her focus to the floor. "Yes…sir."

He wasn't surprised she wasn't comfortable addressing him by his given name. They were strangers, after all. That would come in time.

"Which means…" He brought his attention to the younger child. "You are Arabelle."

The younger girl nodded and inched even nearer to her governess.

"I've asked for a tea tray, my lord," Miss Feathers put in. "I'm sure you're parched from your journey."

Ronan wasn't.

He'd stopped in Rochester. After calling on a few merchants to which Masterson had owed balances and paying those debts, he'd consumed a simple but satisfying meal of stew, cheese, dark bread, and ale at The Hair of the Hog's Pub and Inn.

He'd also had a short but interesting conversation with Cammie Sumner—Masterson's former housemaid. The girl was a brazen, forward chit, full of herself, for sure. Though it had only been just past eleven of the clock, she'd offered to take him upstairs to *discuss* her previous employer.

When she'd realized Ronan wasn't interested in sampling her favors, Miss Sumner had turned petulant. With a toss of her stringy brown hair, she'd planted her reddened hands on her ample hips. An unbecoming sneer marring her pretty face, she said, "I suppose yer like the lieutenant then. The fool preferred that skinny-hipped, holier-than-thou governess, Mercy Feathers."

Several coarsely-attired patrons turned avid gazes in their direction, undoubtedly eager to hear whatever gossip Cammie Sumner bandied about.

"Are you implying Lieutenant Masterson's relationship with Miss Feathers was more than professional in nature?" Ronan had prodded, the fingers of one hand wrapped casually around the pewter tankard.

He took a long sip of the dark, warm ale, observing the girl over the rim.

Jealousy flashed in her eyes.

"Oh, aye, for certain," Miss Sumner said, nodding vehemently. A cunning glint entered those whisky-brown orbs. "I cannot count the number of times I saw her departin' his bedchamber with me own eyes. Though for the life of me, I could never understand what the lieutenant saw in her when he could've had this."

She placed her hands under her voluptuous

breasts, thrusting them dangerously higher until Ronan feared they might spill over the bodice of her simple gown.

"Cammie Sumner!" thundered a harsh male voice as the beefy innkeeper trooped toward her, a scowl wrinkling his broad forehead.

She glowered at her father before grudgingly dropping her mutinous gaze to the well-scrubbed floor.

"Yer mother needs help with the baking." He jabbed a big thumb toward the kitchen. "Go on now, lass."

A pout turning her mouth downward, she flung her hair over her shoulder and flounced away.

"Sorry I am about that, guv. Because Cammie was a maid for Lieutenant Masterson for a time, me daughter has a high opinion of herself. She's always puttin' on haughty airs and such." He tossed a fretful glance toward the kitchen. "She's never been content with her lot or her station."

Another patron signaled the proprietor.

"Excuse me, sir." Mr. Sumner had hurried away.

Ronan pitied the man having to deal with his cheeky daughter. She'd likely end up with a babe and no husband.

"Are we to have lemon cake with tea too?" Miss Arabelle asked eagerly, her big eyes wide and hopeful.

Her question ended Ronan's contemplation of earlier in the day. He wasn't sure where Cammie Sumner fit into this puzzle or how trustworthy the girl was. Therefore, he tucked her conversation into the back of his mind with the other musings about Mercy Feathers for the time being.

Quite a stack of ruminations would need sorting through later.

At Miss Arabelle's innocent question, a becoming flush stole its way up Miss Feathers's porcelain skin. "Not today, darling."

"It's been ever so long since we've had biscuits or cake," Miss Bellamy said, though there was no hint of petulance in her pronouncement. She simply stated a fact she'd come to accept.

"I know, dearest, and I'm sorry. However, I've only asked Mrs. Stanley to prepare tea today." Miss Feathers studiously avoided looking in his direction.

Because they hadn't anything else to offer?

Just how had they managed without funds for two months?

"I'm yet quite full from a robust meal in Rochester, but tea would be appreciated," Ronan fibbed. He far preferred coffee but doubted there was any to be had. He was all the more grateful he'd eaten his fill prior to arriving.

A few minutes later, as they all sat awkwardly around the tea table, steam spiraling upward from the four matching teacups, Ronan cleared his throat.

The lack of milk and sugar to embellish the brew didn't go unnoticed, though his wards seemed unaffected. Mayhap they all preferred their tea plain, but that was unlikely.

Both his sisters as well as Mother enjoyed their tea with milk and a lump of sugar.

"After our tea, Miss Feathers, I should like a private word with you."

Her winged eyebrows arched, but she nodded nonetheless. "Of course, my lord."

Ronan couldn't quite name the color of her hair or her slightly darker eyebrows. Her hair was a collection of golds, honeys, coppers, gingers, bronzes, and flaxen. He flexed his fingers against the urge to remove her hairpins, spread that mass around her shoulders, and run his hands through its luxurious length.

Miss Arabelle puckered her forehead. "Miss Mercy, why do *you* call Mister Ronan my lord?"

Miss Feathers's bow-shaped lips formed a fond smile. "It wouldn't be appropriate for me to address him by his given name. You and Bellamy are his wards…"

Her smile dimmed, and she glanced up, her soft green-eyed gaze asking a pregnant question.

Are you their guardian?

"I am, indeed," Ronan affirmed, and relief flooded her eyes. "I have the documents to prove it too," he said with what was meant as a mischievous wink but only earned him startled, widened eyes from the three females.

"As I was saying, Arabelle, you and Bellamy are his lordship's wards and are of a higher social station than I am," Miss Feathers said gently. "I would never presume to overstep the bounds and address a lord so familiarly. It isn't done."

"Why?" her brow still scrunched, Arabelle looked between Ronan and Miss Feathers. "You permit Bellamy and me to call you Miss Mercy when we should address you as Miss Feathers."

"That's because she's been with us for five years and is part of our family, silly goose," Bellamy announced, giving her sister a superior look. "Miss Mercy has only just met our new guardian, and he only knows her as our governess."

Although Ronan didn't think Bellamy had done so deliberately or meant any offense, clear lines had been drawn.

Mercy Feathers was family.

He, however, was not.

A look of consternation skimmed over Bellamy's features, and her little hand crept toward Miss Feathers's slim fingers. Without hesitation, Miss Feathers took the child's hand in her own.

"She'll remain our governess, won't she, your lordship?" Her voice quavered, and she bit her lower lip. Bellamy lowered her lashes but not before Ronan spied a sheen of moisture there.

She was the more cautious of the two sisters. It was only natural, as Bellamy was the elder that she'd want to protect her sister.

As Sanford has tried to protect you in his own way?

Sanford did mean well, but his own arrogance and conceit often impeded his efforts.

Arabelle thrust her lower lip out. Tears flooded her eyes and dribbled down her cheeks as she gazed frantically back and forth between Ronan and Miss Feathers.

"She will, won't she?" she cried in alarm. "You won't send Miss Mercy away, will you?"

*I have the most excellent news, Mercy. Balderbrook's
Institution for Genteel Young Ladies is opening
another finishing school outside of London in June.
I've been promoted to assistant headmistress at the
new location. We are seeking instructors for nearly
every subject. I've also written Honoria, Grace,
Faith, and Trinity to offer them interviews. If you
Are interested in a position, please respond with
all due haste. We are conducting interviews shortly.*

~ Miss Chasity Noble in a letter to
Miss Mercy Feathers
Sent to Rochester, then forwarded to London—in route

9

*Rochester, England
Masterson's residence study
An hour later*

Hands folded in her lap, Mercy sat docilely and
composed in the armchair situated before
Lieutenant Masterson's desk. She presented what
Hester Shepherd had drilled into her students as the
model of reserved propriety.

The young women of Haven House and Academy
for the Enrichment of Young Women might've been

born into shame and disgrace, but each and every one could conduct herself with the comportment and poise a high-born noblewoman would envy.

Mrs. Shepherd had seen to that.

Lord Ronan Brockman—the epitome of casual repose—relaxed in the prominent chair Mercy had reluctantly used since Lieutenant Masterson's death. It was rather peculiar to see another man behind the mahogany desk, but she supposed she ought to become accustomed to it.

If she was retained as a governess, that was.

Naturally, he'd conduct the estate's business from the study. Unless he planned on delegating that duty to a steward or man of business. Pray God *not* that repugnant toady, Joseph Bralen. She wasn't in a position to object to such an arrangement, yet she could not abide the slimy little man.

Lord Ronan Brockman, on the other hand...

Schooling her face into neutral contours, Mercy took a visual inventory from beneath her lashes.

He was handsome.

Undeniably so.

His scar, though noticeable, wasn't a hideous distraction. He didn't seem self-conscious about the jagged flesh lashing his face either. Mercy had gathered he'd acquired the wound when the lieutenant had saved Brockman's life.

She'd like to hear that story, in truth.

His superfine deep burgundy wool coat did

marvelous things to the rich sun-streaked brown of his hair. Faint stubble shadowed his hewn, square, sun-browned jaw. A jaw which he rested atop one fisted hand as he shamelessly stared at her.

One thing was for certain. The gentleman before her was no soft-skinned, pale-faced dandy. No, indeed. He'd spent time outdoors, and from the breadth of his shoulders and the muscles straining to free themselves of the fabric constraining them, he was accustomed to physical exertion.

Mercy uncrossed and recrossed her ankles, positive he wasn't obtuse but rather was purposely causing her discomfiture with his extended silence.

Why didn't he say something?

"*Ahem.*" She cleared her throat, hoping the impatient noise might prompt him to speak.

It didn't.

He must be aware his present untenable behavior was unconscionably impolite.

Truthfully, if it wasn't for her devotion to Bellamy and Arabelle, she'd give her notice this instant. What an odious man to intentionally cause her disquiet.

The question was, why?

Why was he acting like this?

Had Brockman heard the unsavory rumors in Rochester that her friend Joy Morrisette had warned Mercy about? Righteous anger flickered low in her belly, and she curled her toes to release the tension.

Or had that weasel Mr. Braylen shared his lewd

imaginings with his lordship?

She took a series of three deep breaths and slowly released them to calm herself.

Why must people be so ugly and unkind?

Whispering that she had been the lieutenant's mistress.

Codswallop.

Furthermore, just who had concocted that repugnant tale?

To what purpose?

Well, two could play at this lengthy silence.

A façade of placid serenity, Mercy silently recited the Beatitudes in her head while waiting for his lordship to come to the point of this meeting he'd requested.

Blessed are the poor in spirit, for theirs is the kingdom of heaven.

Outwardly, she appeared composed and the model of decorum. Inwardly, she was a riotous mess, and the crescent half-moons carved into her palms with her fingernails gave testament to that inner turmoil.

Impatience thrumming through her, she tapped the toe of one shoe. Once. Then aghast at her show of pique, she pressed the balls of her feet firmly into her shoes, lest her traitorous toes began tapping once more.

A raging tempest billowed around inside her, and no matter how many calming breaths she took or how many scriptures she silently recited, she feared what this man would say.

Or what she might say in response.

Mercy tightened her clammy palms until the knuckles turned white.

Blessed are those who mourn, for they will be comforted.

It wasn't just her life that lay in the balance.

If it were, Mercy would not be nearly as apprehensive.

Blessed are those who hunger and thirst for righteousness, for they will be filled.

Brockman smiled, his mouth quirking up in that rakish way it had when he'd stood on the stoop and mocked her.

She supposed he practiced that disarming upward sweep of his mouth to charm the ladies. Lovely ladies who, no doubt, batted their eyelashes and gave him coy glances.

As she'd spent no time whatsoever around eligible young men, she wasn't exactly immune to such maneuvers, but neither was she affected by them. It was a game played by those who could afford to waste time—those whose flirtations were as common and expected as the sun's placid journey across the sky each day.

Or so she assured herself.

Blessed are the merciful, for they—

"I shall get straight to the point, Miss Feathers," his lordship said.

Finally.

He rested his elbows on the desktop, and her focus was drawn to the crisp dark curls covering his knuckles. Odd, she'd never noticed the hair on a man's hands before. It only served to emphasize this man's masculine virility.

Stop it, Mercy Augusta Judith Shepard Feathers.

Lord Ronan seemed to peer deep into her soul, a meditative gleam in his keen brown gaze. Not just plain, common brown, but a rich, deep shade like molasses or gingerbread cake.

What?

Molasses? Gingerbread?

Whatever was Mercy thinking?

This stranger held her future in his hands, and she was comparing his eyes to *food*?

A mortified groan tickled the back of her throat.

Swallowing hard, she forced herself to meet Lord Ronan's unwavering gaze.

Was she supposed to say something?

What had he said?

Ah, yes. Something about getting straight to the point.

"Of course, my lord."

"Lieutenant Masterson's estate is bankrupt," he announced succinctly.

Mercy couldn't prevent the small, startled gasp that slipped past her lips, which had parted at his blunt statement.

Bankrupt?

How was that possible?

"This house, its contents, any livestock or cattle, everything will need to be sold to pay his creditors."

"I beg your pardon?" Mercy managed on a croak.

"Masterson mortgaged this house to its stately dormers," Lord Ronan said as smoothly as if he was discussing the weather. "Due to several unwise investments, he was insolvent at the time of his death."

Tappity-tap. Tappity-tap. Tappity-tap.

He drummed his fingertips atop the desk, little finger to index to forefinger in quick succession.

A nasty thought wiggled its way into her mind. Had his lordship hoped to be the guardian of a wealthy, flourishing estate so he might prosper from his new position?

Many guardians did just that.

Oh, merciful heavens.

Why hadn't that thought occurred to Mercy before?

She hadn't known the lieutenant's financial status was so dire. She'd presumed he had funds in a bank and that Lord Ronan would utilize those monies to settle the debts she wasn't authorized to pay.

But Ronan *had* admitted to accepting the official appointment of guardianship. Now he acknowledged he was being saddled with the financial responsibility of Arabelle and Bellamy as well.

Did he resent the added obligation?

At last, she summoned her fortitude. "I see."

What did he expect her to say or do?

Would the girls' possessions also be sold?

She'd heard of such cases. Every item was carefully recorded in a ledger along with its worth right down to children's toys and undergarments.

A bit of the starch went out of her spine at the next unwanted thought.

Would Lord Ronan have the funds to repay her wages?

In truth, she was willing to forgo compensation for a time until Arabelle and Bellamy settled into their new lives. After that, depending on the circumstances, she'd look at her options.

His lordship leaned back, one hand on the desk, idly playing with the quill's feather. He ran his callused thumb back and forth, back and forth across the stiff barbs. "I understand that there are five staff remaining in addition to yourself?"

"No, my lord." Mercy met his gaze without cringing. "Three more resigned their positions last week. All who remain are the cook, Mrs. Deborah Stanley, and the estate gardener who is also acting as a stable hand at present, Felix Norman. They are of an age where it will be difficult for them to find new positions."

Mercy had presented that fact as delicately as possible. She'd fretted about the elderly servants too. They weren't likely to find new positions at their age, and if Lieutenant Masterson's estate was bankrupt, there were no monies for pensions.

"Ah." A frown snapped his lordship's hawkish eyebrows together. He rubbed his jaw as he stared past her. "I shall see to it that Mrs. Stanley and Mr. Norman are pensioned off, if that is what they desire. If not, I'm sure one of my father's many houses could use loyal servants such as them."

She stared at him in shock as a warm feeling fluttered in the vicinity of her chest.

Could Ronan Brockman really be kind *and* handsome?

Perhaps, he wasn't quite the ogre she'd imagined him to be in her mind.

Wait.

Did he have his own funds, or would he impose upon his father's coffers? If so, would the marquess be as generous as his son? It was far easier to spend someone else's money than one's own. And to make promises that he might not be in a position of keeping.

However, Mercy couldn't very well demand to know if he was independently wealthy.

"That would be very benevolent, and I have no doubt they would appreciate your generosity." At least she needn't fret about Mrs. Stanley or Norman any longer. *If* Lord Ronan made good on his promise.

"I should like to return to London the day after tomorrow, Miss Feathers. Does that give you sufficient time to pack Bellamy's and Arabelle's personal possessions?"

He still hadn't mentioned her continued employment.

Angling her head, Mercy gave a succinct nod. "Yes. That is plenty of time."

How would she tell them they'd never set foot in their home again?

She wouldn't.

Not yet, anyway. It would serve absolutely no purpose other than to upset the girls.

Mercy's attention shifted to Lord Ronan tapping the fingers of his right hand upon the desk. He scrutinized her with a thoroughness and concentration that made her want to squirm in her chair.

What did he seek?

Why did she feel like she was on trial?

His gaze turbulent and mouth grim, he abruptly stopped drumming the desktop. Leaning forward, he asked with a directness that stole the breath from her lungs, "Were you Masterson's mistress?"

Dorthea, please do come for tea Thursday the week after next. Ronan will have returned to town, and his wards ought to be settled by then. Bring your darling granddaughters, if you would be so kind. I intend to introduce Arabelle and Bellamy to a few children near their own ages to make them feel more welcome in London.

~ The Marchioness of Trentholm in a
letter to the Countess of Hurtley

10

Still the study of Masterson's residence
Thirty monstrously awkward seconds later

What? *What?*
        Did he just ask…

No. Of course not.

The charged silence in the room fairly sparked with electricity and accusation.

Squinting in confusion, Mercy shook her head as if to clear her ears. She hadn't heard him correctly. No honorable man would ask a woman something so offensive. It was beyond the pale. Especially a man she'd met just over an hour ago.

And yet...the unyielding contours of his visage suggested otherwise.

"I..." she cleared her throat and swallowed the panic fluttering around her ribs. "I beg your pardon?"

Again, that sardonic smile twisted his lordship's mouth, but no humor lit his eyes.

"I believe you heard me perfectly, Miss Feathers." He placed the quill in its brass holder. "I've heard from two reliable sources." He raised two fingers from the desktop. "That you were, in fact, the lieutenant's mistress in addition to the girls' governess."

Mercy couldn't find her tongue to respond this time.

Two people?

Two?

Who? Why?

Mercy might not have much, but she had her dignity and her pride.

Pride goeth before destruction, a haughty spirit before a fall.

Well, this was one fall she was fully prepared to endure. No one, by all the divine powers, *no one* would cast such a vulgar slur upon her reputation and not feel the full extent of her indignant and wholly justified fury.

Drawing herself upright, she slowly stood, every muscle an inexorable lump of tension and suppressed ire. Heart pounding with a thunderous vengeance, she leveled him with a glance intended to smite him to ashes. Never in her life had anyone brought her to the verge of losing her temper so swiftly. Yet this man— nay, this knave—had her seething almost from the moment she'd laid eyes upon him.

His expression guarded, Lord Ronan eyed her as he leaned into the back of the chair. All indolent and arrogant masculinity, he was so bloody sure of himself.

Mercy despised the dastard for his confidence.

"You have no response?" he drawled, his baritone vibrating with droll derision.

Oh, how she wanted to hit him.

Did he expect her to quail under his scowl?

Burst into tears?

Beg for forgiveness?

Mercy would not. She had more mettle than that, by heaven.

Ronan pinched the bridge of his nose as if his head ached.

Good.

Mercy hoped skull-cracking pain crossed his eyes.

"Honestly, Miss Feathers, I expected you'd ring me a peal and vehemently deny the relationship."

His tone was bland, his expression inscrutable.

"I shan't even honor that repulsive suggestion with an answer." Lifting her chin, Mercy said in a voice not quite steady, and she inwardly cursed him for it, "I shall have the girls' possessions packed and mine as well by morning, day after tomorrow. Until that time, I think it best we avoid one another, my lord."

She pointed to a thick burgundy leather volume beside the unopened stack of correspondences.

He briefly took in the ledger before returning his attention to her, one eyebrow quirked archly. In the study's muted afternoon light, the scar slashing his face gave him a sinister appearance. Or perhaps it was the almost sneer curling his lip that caused the illusion, and she barely resisted the impulse to retreat several paces.

"In that ledger, *your lordship*"—she fairly spat the honorific for it had become grossly apparent, this man had no honor—"I have recorded a detailed account of each expenditure I spent *my* personal savings on in order to sustain this household these past two months while we waited for *you* to put in an appearance."

That irritating dark eyebrow rose another inch at her calculated jab.

In surprise? Doubt? Irritation?

She didn't give two bleats of a lamb if she'd offended him.

With his superior air and vile accusation, he'd insulted her. Cast a mark upon her reputation that was not easily removed.

Removed?

Who was she kidding?

Women were ruined by accusations such as those. Never mind that there was no verity in his charge.

Sucking in an unsteady breath, she willed her voice not to wobble.

"I expect full repayment of my monies before I take my leave."

Mercy had never been bold or demanding, but this insufferable bore had all but called her a whore. While he'd been doing God only knew what these past two months, she'd spent her entire savings taking care of *his* responsibilities.

"Naturally," he rejoined smoothly and without hesitation. "I shall repay any monies you expended on behalf of the household as well as compensate you for your delinquent wages."

Well, that was a small blessing, to be sure.

At least Mercy wouldn't be wholly destitute.

"I also thank you for making such a sacrifice," he murmured, his tone far kinder than it had been a minute before.

Though she could detect no sarcasm, Mercy eschewed responding.

Scorching tears stung her eyes at what this meant, and her heart cracked further.

She would not be with Bellamy and Arabelle. She would sooner cut out her own heart.

Neither would she have a coveted letter of recommendation.

Her future had suddenly turned very bleak, indeed.

Hands fisted at her sides, Mercy glared at Ronan, allowing all of the wrath she'd stifled toward him these many weeks to surface. This privileged rotter had just dashed her hopes of staying with Bellamy and Arabelle into a thousand tiny shards.

She feared she would shatter too.

How would she tell them they couldn't be together anymore?

That this stranger was taking them away from her, and they'd very likely never see one another again?

He sighed, his expression softening around his eyes and mouth. Swiping a hand through his pecan-brown locks, he pointed his gaze to the chair Mercy had just vacated.

"Please sit down, Miss Feathers."

Though it wasn't really a request, lips pressed into two hard lines, she shook her head. She was on the verge of tears, and she'd be hanged if she gave him the satisfaction of weeping in front of him.

"I think not," she snapped between stiff lips, not caring that she was impertinent.

What would his lordship do?

Dismiss her? That was already imminent.

"I shall take my leave and begin packing," she said, already swiveling toward the door.

And seize a few more priceless hours with her precious charges before all of their lives were further devastated.

"No one mentioned you were mule-headed, taxing, and uncompromising," Lord Ronan muttered beneath his breath. "*Not* traits one generally seeks in a governess."

Ooh, the rotten wretch.

Mercy clamped her teeth together against a very, *very* unladylike oath and muscled the retort down.

God rot the clodpoll.

He would expect a biddable, tractable, and docile mouse of a governess. In fact, he probably thought all women ought to be compliant, worshipful, obedient bacon brains.

She jutted her chin up another mutinous inch, her glare blistering as she mentally impaled him.

Do your worst, you pompous prig, she silently challenged, her gaze dueling with his.

Shaking his head, the merest hint of a smile teasing the corners of his molded mouth, Lord Ronan rose and came around the desk. Arms folded across his impossibly broad chest, he rested his slim hips against the edge of the desk before crossing his ridiculously long legs at the ankle.

"I apologize, Miss Feathers. This wasn't the direction I meant for this conversation to go." He glanced up from studying his crossed ankles. Or mayhap it was the pattern on the carpet that caught his attention. "I generally give people the benefit of the doubt and presume their innocence."

Well, thank you very much.

"And *I* am the exception?" she clipped out, standing her ground.

Nevertheless, every fiber of her being screamed for her to turn tail and run from the room. To put as much distance as she could between herself and this aggravating man. Her breaths came in shallow little rasps, and the knot in her middle tightened further, making her sick at her stomach.

Or perchance that was because she hadn't eaten anything since last evening.

"You were seen leaving Lieutenant Masterson's bedchamber," Ronan stated quietly, his tone almost soothing.

What?

How could he possibly know that?

Cammie Sumner.

Oh, the horrid, despicable, jealous, mean-spirited vindictive wretch.

If she were present, Mercy might very well be tempted to slap her smug face.

Very, *very* hard.

Forget the "turn the other cheek" rot. There were times when a person needed to take a stand and call evil for what it was. And Cammie Sumner was a spawn of Satan.

This aristocratic churl already believed the worst of her. Nonetheless, he wouldn't cow her. Mercy would not grovel and insist he'd been misinformed.

It would make no difference, in any event, she felt sure.

She'd wager her virtue Lord Ronan Brockman had made his mind up about her before he'd ever seen or spoken to her.

Mercy raised a derisive eyebrow as if to say, "So what if I was?"

"On numerous occasions, I might add," his lordship clarified in a neutral tone. His stern gaze was anything but. Condemnation and indictment glittered in that searing dark honey-brown gaze.

He'd passed judgment and found her guilty based on a jealous chit's spiteful tattle. Was this the kind of man Bellamy and Arabelle would be raised by? One who didn't bother to learn facts but listened to contrived *on dit?*

Mercy fisted her hands to keep from launching herself at him and either wrapping them around his thick neck or clocking him in his too-perfect aristocratic nose. His continued lazy contemplation—that dashed sarcastic smile and single dark brow shied upward—only fanned her fury. Never before in her life had Mercy felt such scorching rage or the violent urge to attack someone.

In the very brief time she'd known Ronan, she'd come to an undeniable and finite conclusion. She did *not* like the man. That *he* should be assigned the care of Arabelle and Bellamy seemed the quintessence of a cruel jest.

"Have you nothing to say in your defense?" his lordship queried, a jot less sarcastically but terse nonetheless.

Mindful of his probing stare, she lifted a shoulder nonchalantly and brushed a strand of hair off her forehead.

"I suppose that's the top and bottom of it—the

truth dwindled to a nutshell. I *was* in the lieutenant's chamber," she glibly agreed. Almost tauntingly and disdainfully. "Many, *many* times, in truth."

"So you *admit* to the indiscretion?" Shock pitched his lordship's voice louder and crinkled the corners of his eyes, gone stormy as a tempest at sea.

Hysterical laughter bubbled up her throat, and an indelicate sound somewhere between a laugh and a snort passed her lips. He'd listened to gossip and wrongly accused her of being immoral, and now he was confounded by her admission?

The rotter couldn't have it both ways.

"I was in Lieutenant Masterson's bedchamber any number of times, my lord. So many, in point of fact, that I long ago lost count."

Make of that what you will.

He cleared his throat, appearing completely nonplussed.

Allowing an imitation of his contemptuous smile to sweep the edges of her mouth upward, Mercy leaned forward and nodded. If she was to be sacked, she might as well have her say and put the odious oaf in his place.

"Always, *always,* my lord, after finding the girls' *cat* asleep atop the lieutenant's bed, and never, *never* when *he* was at home."

"Jesus," Brockman swore beneath his breath while rubbing two fingers across his forehead. "I…"

She gave vent to her scorn and laughed.

"I bet your *reliable* sources forgot to mention those little insignificant details, didn't they?" She raked her gaze over him in scathing contempt. "Gossip is a peculiar thing, your lordship. It makes those who believe it appear as much the fool as those bandying unfounded rumors about."

Lord knew she ought to care that she'd just called him a fool but by Hades...

How dare he?

Mercy blinked rapidly against the rush of tears pooling in her eyes. Taking a deep breath, she pinched her eyes shut for another breath. She must reign her temper in.

His countenance a combination of chagrin and remorse, Ronan stood to his full, impressive height. He must be at least two inches over six feet, making Mercy feel even shorter than her five feet four inches.

"Miss Feathers, I..."

Mercy threw a hand up, palm extended, and beyond caring about decorum and propriety and all that other politesse claptrap.

"Save your pretty speech, my lord. I have two little girls whose lives have been thrown into further tumult who need me. Somehow, I have to prepare them to leave the only home they've ever known to go live with a stranger."

Heeding a modicum of wisdom, she decided against pointing out that that stranger had taken his sweet time coming to see them as well.

"What's more," she said, "I must somehow tell them I shan't be with them to ease that godawful transition. If you cannot try to put yourself in their place, my lord, I can! I know only too well how incomprehensibly unbearable this will be for them."

An errant tear slipped from the corner of her eye, and she angrily swept it away.

"Mercy," Ronan said, drawing nearer and cupping her shoulders, his gaze probing hers. "I am heartily sorry. I believe I have misjudged you, and I beg your forgiveness."

And then, to her utter and complete horror, Mercy couldn't hold back the tears she'd stifled all these months. The dam broke, and choking sobs escaped her as huge, scalding droplets poured from her eyes.

She slapped a palm over her mouth and had turned to race from the room when Lord Ronan drew her into his arms, pressing her into that marble-like wall of a chest that smelled splendidly of sandalwood, starch, and mint. Mayhap even a whiff of evergreen or eucalyptus.

What did Mercy do?

Did she fight his embrace?

Berate him for taking liberties?

Kick his shins or scratch his face?

No. No, indeed.

Mercy sank into that soothing enclosure and, clinging to him, wept as if her heart was broken.

For the sake of my wards, I am retaining their current governess. At least for the time being. I'll explain more when I return to London. I found Miss Feathers's letter of recommendation amongst Masterson's papers from a Mrs. Hester Shepherd of Haven House and Academy for the Enrichment of Young Women located in Essex. Might I impose upon you to use your considerable influence to look into the establishment and Mrs. Shepherd for me? Miss Feathers seems vaguely familiar, as if we've met before, thoug I know that is implausible.

~ Ronan Brockman, in a letter to his father,
the Marquess of Trentholm

11

*The outskirts of London
10 March 1818
Early evening*

Oxonian hat low on his forehead and arms folded across his greatcoat, Ronan unabashedly observed Mercy, as he'd come to think of her. The sun, muted by plumy clouds, balanced low on the rosy-orange horizon, as the well-sprung coach trundled onward.

Their departure had been delayed by several days.

Initially, Ronan had thought to leave the disbursement of Masterson's estate in Joseph Bralen's hands. However, what little respect he'd had for the solicitor went up in a wisp of cindery ashes after Ronan had learned of Mercy's innocence.

Instead, he'd contacted his man of business and asked him to meet Ronan in Rochester.

That, of course, also meant posting a letter to his father explaining his delay in returning with his wards. It required a missive to Mr. Bralen terminating his services too.

A satisfied smile inched Ronan's mouth up on one side.

The slimy solicitor had sought to see Mercy discharged and instead found himself sacked.

Justice, swift and appropriate, Ronan thought.

Besides, the man rubbed him the wrong way, and after he'd disparaged Mercy, Ronan itched to wring his scrawny neck. He refused to work with anyone lacking integrity and common decency. Bralen had quite obviously dispensed with both qualities decades earlier, despite his self-appointed piety.

Once his man of affairs, Basil Kline, had arrived, Ronan had set about pensioning off Mrs. Stanley and Mr. Norman. Both servants had agreed to stay on until the livestock, house, and contents were sold.

Ronan had spared Mercy the task of explaining to Arabelle and Bellamy that they wouldn't be returning to their home. He assured Mercy he would inform the girls once they were in London. The past several hours, however, as they put more and more distance between them and Rochester, he'd wondered if that had been a wise decision.

Shouldn't he have allowed Bellamy and Arabelle a chance to say goodbye to their home? Their horses and servants?

He grimaced.

Blister it.

What did he know of what was best for little girls?

God help him. And them.

Ronan wasn't a particularly religious man. Yes, he attended church on Sunday as most of the *ton* was wont to do. It was expected, just as using the correct fork and spoon while dining was. However, the hypocrisy he witnessed on a nearly daily basis among the upper ten thousand made it tough to take to heart anything preached from the pulpit.

He well knew that sitting in a pew Sunday morning did not a Christian make. How many of those in their finery, eyes heavy with boredom, had dallied with someone other than their spouse the night before?

Gambled away a fortune?

Drunk themselves into a stupor?

Cheated or swindled or gossiped?

Nonetheless, Ronan permitted his eyelids to drift shut and offered up a simple prayer.

Lord, I need your help. I have no idea what I am

doing, but I want what is best for Bellamy and Arabelle. Please guide me.

Feeling oddly at peace, he opened his eyes, and his attention fixated on Mercy.

Something undefinable cinched behind his breastbone.

What was it about her that muddled him?

The fading light played across the sweep of her cheek as the coach wheels ground along the well-traveled road. Her profile and delicate features suggested she was a woman of genteel breeding.

Again, that impression of having seen her before niggled in a fusty recess of his mind.

It wasn't possible.

She'd told him herself that her first and only position was as Masterson's governess. Masterson had hired her directly from that odd school Ronan had asked his father to poke around about. Furthermore, Mercy had never been to London, and Ronan had never been to Rochester before.

He'd heard somewhere at some time that everyone had a double someplace in the world. Ronan wasn't positive he bought into that myth, but he couldn't rule it out entirely either.

After her emotional outburst in the study, she had retreated into a shell of respectability and decorum. Her outrage hadn't been feigned, nor had her wounded pride. If he hadn't believed her then, which he had, it had taken less than four-and-twenty hours in the house to realize she hadn't lied.

Mercy Feathers was clever, resourceful, and determined, but Ronan was convinced that she was incapable of dissembling. Another stab of guilt elbowed him hard in the ribs and abraded his pride. At this rate, his regret would see him bruised and bloodied, his remorse chafed and scoured raw.

To alleviate that discomfit, Ronan considered what he might've done right amid this new reality that was his life. He'd taken it upon himself to sort through his friend's possessions and save any items he thought the girls might want of their father's. He'd also purchased the family portraits and had left Mr. Kline instructions to have them sent to London.

In point of fact, he doubted Mercy capable of perfidy or duplicity.

Again, he surreptitiously studied her.

What would his family make of her?

He'd soon know.

Another thirty minutes or so and he'd introduce his sweet wards and their pretty governess to his parents, siblings, and the staff. For reasons he couldn't quite put his finger on, Ronan was reluctant to do the latter.

It made no sense. It was ludicrous, in fact.

He couldn't summon a solitary rational cause for the disinclination.

After all, Mercy would be a part of the Trentholm household whether she or he wanted it otherwise.

Not that he didn't want her there.

His wards did, which meant he did. He rather thought the devoted governess would go wherever they went. Ronan also resolutely believed, after that tragic scene in the study, Mercy would rather be anywhere he wasn't.

Guilt and contrition had buffeted him for days after she'd dissolved into tears in the study. She'd been mortified at her display. He'd been eviscerated that he'd caused her distress—his only thought to ease the pain he'd so callously inflicted.

"Always, always, my lord, after finding the girls' cat asleep atop the lieutenant's bed, and never, never when he was at home."

As each word paraded through his memory, the lash of a whip sliced his soul.

Hounds' teeth.

He'd bloody-well botched that interview or whatever one wanted to call the ill-fated conversation. Served him right for leaping to conclusions and bending his ear toward tattle. He'd witnessed Fluffer-Muffer sleeping on Lieutenant Masterson's bed with his own eyes.

You did ask her to explain herself.

Yes, after asking point-blank if she was Masterson's mistress.

A groan scrambled around the back of his throat.

It was to Mercy's credit that she hadn't slapped his face and left the premises that very afternoon. He'd learned, of course, her dedication to Arabelle and Bellamy wouldn't permit her to abandon them, even if she'd wanted to spite him. And it wasn't as if employment opportunities were prolific for young women—particularly without a letter of reference.

What was more, according to her own testimony, she'd been without funds.

He'd rectified that wrong posthaste.

Mercy had only graced him with an infinitesimal nod when he'd paid her back wages and reimbursed her expenses the next day after examining the ledgers. Meticulous and detailed, she'd accounted for every pence spent. He'd not have been able to stretch those monies to the degree she had.

In truth, Miss Mercy Feathers was turning out to be a much more complex female than he'd anticipated. In short, he wasn't certain what to do with her and fully intended to grovel if he must and ask his mother to take over supervising the governess.

After all, Mother knew precisely what every other servant in the household was up to at any given minute. She'd dealt with governesses for her daughters. Surely, it made sense that she would take on the responsibility of Miss Feathers too.

Mayhap his mother and sisters would introduce Mercy to London when they toted Arabelle and Bellamy about town. Surely governesses accompanied their charges on such excursions. For he hadn't a doubt that Mother would delight in furnishing the girls with new wardrobes.

Yes, yes, indeed. That was precisely what Ronan would do.

Trailing the length of his scar with his forefinger, he cursed inwardly.

Except—*blast it to Hades*—he knew in his gut that Mother wouldn't alleviate him of the responsibility. And there was the deuced rub. For whatever unfathomable reason, his lovable but sometimes immensely bothersome family was conspiring against him in this matter. Probably nothing more than very poorly disguised attempts to keep him in England.

Ronan didn't like not feeling in command of himself—his emotions, his purpose, his future, his actions. Regardless, he strongly suspected every last one of those was no longer under his control.

Heaving a sigh worthy of Marissa's dramatics, Ronan eyed the basket from whence peeved rustling sounds emerged regularly for the past several minutes.

Slicing Mercy a side-eyed glance, he was relieved to see she hadn't seemed to notice his sigh. Or if she had, she chose to do what any servant worth their salt did. Ignore their employer's indiscretions, idiosyncrasies, and failings.

As she had throughout the journey, Fluffer-Muffer made a harsh, drawn-out disgruntled noise—somewhere between an annoyed yowl and an infuriated hiss. As if the cat wanted to ensure the humans understood just how inconvenienced and put upon she was for having to endure the journey stuffed in a hamper like a sausage in a too-small casing.

Since the contentious cat favored him more than either of his new and still leery and suspicious wards, the only vacant spot in the coach after he'd handed Mercy and the girls in early this morning had been next to the miffed feline's basket.

Had he been alone in the coach, Ronan would've stretched his legs and propped them on the opposite seat. At the last inn, while the team was exchanged, he had stretched his legs and taken several turns around the courtyard. Nonetheless, his muscles had protested for the past hour about the immobility.

Across the coach, Mercy presented the quintessence of decorous behavior against the backdrop of the claret-colored squabs. Nothing in her mien hinted at the spitfire who had so soundly put him in his place but a few days ago.

Which was the real Mercy Feathers?

Perhaps a mélange of both?

She wore the same unremarkable black bonnet and gray cloak he'd first met her in. With her hair and eyes, she would be resplendent in greens and corals, blues and teals. Except, he supposed, governesses weren't permitted anything brighter than a staid dark blue.

Pity that.

Flanking her, Arabelle and Bellamy slept on, their heads resting on Mercy's thighs. One of her gloved hands rested on each girl's shoulder in what could only be described as a maternal gesture. Whenever the girls stirred, she idly smoothed her palms over their backs in another nurturing motion.

The instinct was so natural that Ronan doubted she was even aware she calmed his wards. If ever a woman was born to be a mother, it was Miss Mercy Feathers.

Where in God's holy name had *that* thought come from?

The tip of Mercy's little finger on her left hand peeked through her glove. Ronan was no fashion expert, but he'd wager his mother and sisters would have a fit of the vapors at the condition of her obviously hand-knitted—*and mended*—gloves.

Not that Mother or Corinna or Marissa were snobs.

Well, perhaps they were. Not deliberately, however.

For sure, they'd never gone without—anything. Furthermore, neither Ronan's mother nor his sisters would ever have been able to keep the Masterson household functioning for two months on a governess's wages.

Neither could *he* have done.

The coach hit a particularly deep rut in the road, bouncing him against the door. Mercy braced her feet on the floor, which she barely reached, and wedged herself firmly into the squabs while stabilizing the sleeping girls.

Other than a little "Oomph," she remained silent.

Another thing to respect about Miss Mercy Feathers. She did not complain. Not once the entire journey. This enchanting governess was stoic and intrepid.

Neither girl stirred on her lap, and Ronan envied the sleep of youth.

Since his early morn summons to Pelandale House, he hadn't slept through the night.

Sniffing slightly, he rubbed the side of his nose, which had itched like the dickens most of the journey, giving him cause to speculate that he might be allergic to cats. Or perhaps a spring-blooming tree or bush on Masterson's estate caused his symptoms.

In truth, until the past couple of days, he'd never spent any time around felines.

His father owned dogs—eight Sussex spaniels which he kept at his country seat. The marquess firmly believed hunting hounds and felines did not mix. Hence, Ronan had never spent any lengthy time in the vicinity of gray furballs with scissor-like teeth and talon-like claws. And eyes that fairly charred a person with their displeasure.

Though, to be fair, Fluffer-Muffer hadn't directed any unpleasant behaviors toward him. Instead, the beast made a blasted nuisance of herself with her persistent determination to make sure she was never more than two feet from Ronan at any given time.

His wards found the cat's intense and immediate attachment to him jolly good fun. More than once, they'd burst into giggles, quickly hidden behind their little hands, at the cat's besotted behavior. Alas, their governess found the cat's infatuation highly amusing as well. Although Mercy concealed her twitching lips with an alacrity, he couldn't help but appreciate.

That was, if he weren't trying to dislodge the cat from his lap, his shoulder, his boots...and his bed.

As he'd learned, thereby further strengthening Mercy's defense, the cat had a distinct penchant for gentlemen's beds. Not once, however, had Mercy come in search of the purring cat in his bedchamber.

Eyes bright with keen interest and her face serene, she peered out the window at the passing scenery. The changing light cast shadows over her face, softening the tension-etched brackets around her full, pretty mouth and easing the creases between her red-blond eyebrows.

"Is this your first time coming up to London, Miss Feathers?"

Was he daft?

He knew it was. Mercy had told him as much.

She started and faced him, her gaze questioning and perhaps the merest bit satirical.

"Yes, my lord. As I said previously, I've only ever lived in Rochester and Essex."

The heat of a full-on flush skated up his neck from his cravat to his hairline.

My God.

He was blushing. Actually blushing. Like a wet-behind-the eyes whelp.

When was the last time he'd turned red in the face?

Ah, yes.

Ronan remembered the precise ill-fated time—at the Wimpletons' annual summer house party. Much to his boyish consternation, he had come upon a very plump couple *cavorting* near the pond where he'd gone to search for frogs.

Some things could not be unseen. Even over twenty years later, Ronan had to blink and shake his head to dislodge that staggering—*bloody dashed terrifying to a seven-year-old*—vision.

"I think you will enjoy London." Ronan plowed onward. In for a penny and all that. "There are several parks and museums you might visit with the girls. The Egyptian Hall at Bullock's Museum is particularly fascinating. I believe Arabelle and Bellamy would also enjoy Astley's Amphitheater and, of course, Vauxhall Gardens and Hatchards."

"Hatchards?" Mercy did that cute thing of scrunching her brows together, which meant she was either thinking or confused.

"It's a bookstore. Temple of the Muses is another rather impressive bookstore. Naturally, Arabelle and Bellamy must visit Gunter's Tea Shop for ices." He slung his ankle over his knee and began tapping his fingertips on his thigh. "I'm positive my mother and sisters will have several outings planned in short order."

A smile bent her rose-bud mouth upward, and curiosity danced in her eyes, the color of plane tree leaves at the moment. "How many sisters have you, my lord?"

"Two half-sisters." He held up two buff-colored gloved fingers. "Corrina and Marissa, both younger than I. Marissa is sixteen, and Corrina is two-and-twenty going on forty. She's quite droll and doesn't much care for decorum."

Her smile widened at his description. "She sounds fascinating."

"Yes, well. In truth, Corrina is frequently quite shocking. My mother despairs of her ever behaving like a proper lady."

What would Miss Mercy Feathers make of his hellion of a sister?

"Are they your only siblings?" Mercy asked.

"No." Ronan shook his head as the unmistakable sounds of purring emanated from the basket. Naturally, after seven hours, the temperamental creature had finally decided to settle down.

"I also have two brothers. One three years older and another two years younger." He chuckled. "Sanford and Benjamin couldn't be any more different than night and day. Sanford, the next marquess, is terribly solemn and serious while Benjamin thinks life is a lark."

Except for that business about meeting someone special that Benjamin had mentioned last week. Before

Ronan could ask him to elucidate on the matter, Sanford had interrupted them enjoying a brandy in the library.

With a silent warning, more of a pleading with his eyes for Ronan to discontinue the discussion, Ben had abruptly changed the subject to an upcoming horse race.

Mercy cocked her head, that ugly bonnet giving her the faintest look of a curious little black hen. "And who are you most like?"

Grinning, Ronan winked. "Why, Miss Feathers, I am the perfect balance of both brothers, their unpleasant traits aside, that is."

She raised a skeptical eyebrow but didn't contest his appraisal of himself. Probably because servants couldn't speak freely. Corrina would've told him to sod off or go bugger himself. Both vulgar expressions would've sent their mother into a swoon.

"Have you any sisters or brothers?" Ronan asked amiably, the silence inside the coach of the past few hours having grown tedious.

Mercy's countenance closed as assuredly as if she'd slammed a window shut and then slid the bar home to block any possible intruders.

"My story is not edifying nor uncommon. I have no family, my lord."

Her tone and the immediate presentation of her profile clearly indicated the conversation was at an end. Only Ronan wasn't ready to let it go. Some devil on his shoulder prodded him onward.

"I'm sorry," he murmured. His family might drive him to distraction, but they were a loving lot. Ronan couldn't imagine being alone in the world.

"Orphaned then?" he persisted, aware he crossed the mark into impoliteness.

"Something like that," she said after an interminable pause, her expression inscrutable.

Either Mercy Feathers was an orphan, or she was not. There was no in-between. However, her obvious reserve made him bite his tongue. That discussion could wait for another time.

"We should arrive within a few more minutes," he tried again conversationally. "I'm famished. Mother is certain to have hot baths at the ready for all of us, and I'll wager something delectable to eat."

"Lord Ronan. I highly doubt the marchioness will think it necessary to have a bath and meal prepared for a governess." Her tone held neither reprimand nor disrespect. She was simply reminding him of her station...neither part of the family nor a domestic servant. Governesses occupied an awful place between both, which meant they were never really included or embraced by either.

It must be a wholly lonely existence.

Before Ronan finished his troubling musings, the coach lumbered to a stop before Pelandale House. At once, a footman in spotless crimson and black livery opened the door and set a step stool before the coach.

Ronan climbed down as Mercy woke the girls.

Blinking sleepily, Arabelle and Bellamy permitted him to assist them from the equipage. Mercy stepped from the vehicle before he could turn back to hand her down.

Had she assumed she should disembark on her own? She acted as if governesses were secondary citizens, for pity's sake. He'd treat her with the same respect that he would any female.

Only Ronan had already proven that to be a lie.

At once, the girls each seized her hands, their big brown eyes wary but inquisitive.

"Let's go inside, shall we?" Mercy said softly to encourage them forward to where Ronan waited.

They filed past him, up the steps, and into the manor house.

Ronan followed behind.

"Welcome home, my lord," Sturges said. He turned to Mercy and the girls and gave a noble dip of his head. "Welcome to Pelandale House. I am Sturges."

"Thank you," Ronan replied perfunctorily, pondering why his family wasn't stampeding down the corridors to the foyer.

Mother and Father only had so much control over his three younger siblings. On the other hand, Sandford would never stoop so low as to rush, hurry, scramble, clamber, or any other verb which indicated haste and lack of self-possession.

"Thank you, Sturges," Mercy said in her husky contralto that caused something to unwind in Ronan's middle. "This is Miss Bellamy Masterson and her sister, Arabelle."

"It is a pleasure, Miss Bellamy and Miss Arabelle." The severe planes of the butler's face softened into a warm smile. "The staff have awaited your arrival with great anticipation."

The girls exchanged slightly less suspicious glances and even managed timid smiles.

Sturges could charm the blue out of the sky if he put his mind to it.

"Come, let's see you out of your coats, shall we?" Mercy said.

As the females divested themselves of their outerwear, Ronan shrugged out of his greatcoat. "Are they in the drawing room?"

"Yes, my lord." Sturges extended his hand for Ronan's coat.

Ronan knew full well his family was aware he'd returned. Surprisingly, they hadn't descended upon the new arrivals like winter fog on the River Thames. But then again, Mother would understand how overwhelming this was for Bellamy and Arabelle and had likely insisted on decorum.

He'd be bound that someone would defy her and bolt, however.

Mercy smoothed a hand over her gorgeous hair,

the golden, bronze hues shimmering in the candlelight. The tidy chignon remained undisturbed by the hours of travel and her bonnet.

She summoned a brave smile for her charges. "Shall we go meet Lord Ronan's family?"

"Sweet Jesus," Corrina exclaimed.

As one, they turned toward her.

That was one bet Ronan would've won had he placed a wager.

Her gaze trained on Mercy, his sister gaped. Pointing rudely, she blinked several times as if she couldn't believe what she was seeing. "She's the spitting image of Adelhied Tyndal."

Who in blazes is Adelhied Tyndal?

"Who?" Ronan screwed his face into a frown while sending Mercy a puzzled sidelong glance. He racked his memory, trying to recall the woman.

"Lady Amhurst?" Corinna coaxed. "You've attended several of the same social functions over the years."

A haunted glint entering her tumultuous fern-green eyes, Mercy had gone waxen. She drew the girls nearer and dropped her gaze to the glossy flower-patterned parquet floor.

His sister narrowed her eyes in exasperation as if he were an imbecile for not knowing who Lady Amhurst was. "Really, Ronan. Lady Amhurst is the Duke of—"

"That is quite enough, Corinna," Mother said, a thread of steel in her tempered tone. Their mother's curt admonishment brooked no argument. What was more, it was a rare thing indeed for her to raise her voice.

The gaze she turned on Ronan warned him to hold *his* tongue as well.

What the devil? Something was too smoky by far.

*I do so appreciate the offer, Chasity, but I cannot bring
myself to leave the children. Lord and Lady Ceddes
neglect them dreadfully, barely taking the time to come
down to the country seat twice annually and then only
for a fortnight. The Ceddes are vain, contrary, and
vexingly difficult on a good day. For certain, I would
be better off teaching at Balderbrook's Institution
for Genteel Ladies. Pomeroy is off to Harrow next
year, and the Ceddes have mentioned sending
the girls abroad. Perhaps I can come then
if a position is still available.*

~ Miss Purity Mayfield in a letter
to Miss Chasity Noble

12

*Pelandale House
Mercy's bedchamber
Three hours later*

Mercy wasn't sure how she managed to get
through the past three hours with her poise and
dignity intact.

*Pluck, fortitude, and pure mulish determination.
That is how.*

The charming chamber, more befitting a welcome
guest than a governess, had taken her quite by surprise.

Indeed, her room at Masterson's had been comfortable, and she'd lacked for nothing. Nonetheless, that bedchamber had clearly been intended for a servant.

This delightful room with its cream background silk wallpaper that was covered in ferns and flower sprays, the plush green velvet draperies suspended on brass rosettes and held back with a matching silk cord, and the thickest Aubusson carpet she'd ever stood upon provided the perfect backdrop for the rosewood empire furnishings.

In truth, she felt more like an honored visitor than an employee.

Lying on her back upon her deliciously soft mattress—it felt as if she rested upon a fluffy cloud—topped with a floral yellow, ivory, and green coverlet, she closed her eyes and pressed a palm to her pounding forehead.

Headaches rarely inconvenienced her. In fact, she couldn't recall the last time she'd been afflicted by one. Rubbing little circles with her fingertips upon each temple, she attempted to ease the thrumming.

She could only suppose it was the strain of a long day's travel and being thrust into a new household. Pointedly avoiding looking at Ronan as much of the journey as possible while her stomach roiled with tension and nerves had strained her to the extreme too.

After Lady Trentholm had shushed her flabbergasted daughter, the kind woman had ushered Mercy and the girls into the drawing room and politely inquired about the journey. The whole while, Mercy was very aware of the concert of six gazes studying her with uncanny scrutiny, including Ronan.

Naturally, she'd dredged up her equanimity and pretended Lady Corinna's openmouthed outburst hadn't shaken Mercy to her toes. It had, of course. She'd be a self-deceiving fool to deny it.

It had also raised questions. Lots of questions.

Duke of who?

Who was this Adelhied Tyndal?

Why had Lady Trentholm interrupted her daughter?

Did Ronan know?

More on point, would Mercy ever know?

Did she *want* to?

Ignorance might be bliss, but living in denial and avoiding the truth…

Which was worse?

Again, another question, and entirely pointless at this juncture. At this moment, nothing was to be done, so further fretting was useless. Only the Good Lord knew what it all meant, and she'd simply have to trust Him.

Mercy ceased rubbing her temples and turned onto her side.

Ronan's family was exactly as he'd described them. His father and stepmother epitomized genial nobility—regal, welcoming, and friendly, but not overly so. Perhaps a mite more cordial to the girls than

Mercy, as was appropriate.

After all, she was a mere employee, no different than the dozens of others in their employ. Arabelle and Bellamy were their beloved middle son's new wards and, Mercy supposed, after a fashion, proxy granddaughters.

Pinching the bridge of her nose, Mercy closed her eyes and breathed in and out slowly as she mentally inventoried Ronan's siblings. All were attractive—arrestingly so, truth be told—but that was where their similarities ended.

The largest and darkest in coloring of the brothers, Sanford, was severe to the point of moroseness. Benjamin was fairer than Ronan and cocksure, carefree, and confident.

Marissa, a pale blonde beauty with just a trace of baby fat, was sweet but inclined to dither on about frivolities. She could also be quite melodramatic. Such shallowness might be forgiven. She was only sixteen, after all.

Also possessing light blonde hair and pale, pale blue eyes, Corinna was every bit as gregarious and outspoken as Ronan had promised. From the keen interest in her avid gaze, she was dying to finish saying what her mother had succinctly cut off in the foyer.

Nonetheless, she held her tongue, though Mercy was positive that the instant she left the room, a chaotic discussion would erupt amongst the family.

About her. *And* the unknown duke of somewhere. Mustn't forget him.

It unnerved her to no end. Just one more thing to add to the tangled knot of anxiety and insecurity that had become her life of late.

Still attired in her traveling costume—an unpretentious nut-brown affair—she glanced at the filagree bedside clock, atop of which perched two chubby birds.

Half-past nine.

Perhaps she ought to check on the girls one more time before retiring herself.

In point of fact, this was their first night in their new home.

Mercy had eaten a delicious dinner of ham, seasoned potatoes, peas and carrots, followed by a scrumptious treacle with Bellamy and Arabelle. After their baths, she'd read a chapter from *Gulliver's Travels*.

Both girls loved stories about traveling to exotic places. Their father had enjoyed nothing better than sharing fabulous tales about his adventures as an officer in the navy.

Mercy thought perhaps their next book might be *Robinson Crusoe* or *The Travels of Marco Polo,* or mayhap even *Don Quixote* or *The Adventures of Roderick Random*—although the girls might be a tad young for the latter two novels.

Inhaling a lungful of air, she levered upright, pleased when her head didn't topple from her neck and roll across the carpet.

There.

That wasn't so bad.

The intolerable pounding had subsided to an annoying cadence behind her left eye.

She would check on the girls and then return to her chamber and bathe.

To her surprise, the housekeeper, Mrs. Webber, insisted a bath be prepared for Mercy after the family's. Mrs. Webber had apologized as she showed Mercy to her chambers two doors down from the nursery. "I regret it will likely be ten of the clock, Miss Feathers."

Honestly, Mercy disliked inconveniencing the staff.

"I'd be perfectly content with a basin and a pitcher of warm water, Mrs. Webber," Mercy had said. Although a bath sounded heavenly, waiting until ten to indulge did not. Not only was she exhausted from the journey, but Bellamy and Arabelle were also early risers. They rarely slept past the stroke of six.

Mrs. Webber shook her head so vehemently that the chatelaine at the housekeeper's waist jangled. "None of that. Lord Ronan gave the direction himself. I could not defy him."

He had?

"His lordship insisted you'd be sore after the journey," Mrs. Webber put in with a benevolent smile.

"Oh. Well, in that case, I would be ever so grateful," Mercy conceded. She'd not see the staff rebuked because of her.

That gave Mercy half an hour to check on the girls and finish unpacking.

She let herself out of her bedchamber and walked the short distance to Arabelle and Bellamy's room along the thick carpet. The Brockman's certainly liked their carpets.

A lone sconce lit the hallway, casting weird shadows along its length.

Slipping inside the girls' chamber, she breathed a relieved sigh. They were fast asleep, the fire banked in the grate, and the lamp turned down on a table beneath a window—just as she'd left it. Once she'd checked on each girl and kissed them atop their downy heads, she wandered to the window and pushed the draperies aside.

Even in this prestigious neighborhood, a myriad of foreign city sounds carried to her. London was far different than Rochester. Bigger. Noisier. Faster-paced. Less friendly. The pinnacle of High Society.

This was home now.

But for how long?

Mercy had no way of knowing.

Ronan might decide to do what Purity's employers, Lord and Lady Ceddes, contemplated doing and send the girls off to school. Naturally, she would strenuously advise against such a thing. Regardless, in the end, Mercy had little influence and no control over what happened to Bellamy and Arabelle.

She thrust her chin out and straightened her shoulders.

Well then, she'd just have to make sure the girls wiggled their ways into Ronan's and his family's hearts the way they had hers. Then no one would consider sending them away.

As she turned to leave the nursery, her heart launched to her throat. A large shadow darkened the open doorway for two blinks before Ronan slipped inside.

Upon spying Mercy, he smiled and advanced toward her. "I see they've fallen asleep," he whispered, the sound tickling her ears. "I worried they might be too overwrought to relax and was prepared to send for warm milk."

"That was very thoughtful of you," Mercy whispered in return.

Would this man never cease to surprise her? He actually came to check on the girls' wellbeing himself? Many, many aristocratic parents did no such thing. Those tasks were delegated to servants.

Ronan whisked his appreciative gaze over her, a glint of something a mite more than professional approval in the dark brown depths.

Making a dramatically rueful face more appropriate for a precocious adolescent, he placed his hand over his heart. "I confess, it was my mother's suggestion. I'd never have thought of it. She's quite taken with the girls already."

"I'm glad. I understand what a disruption this is to your life and your family's as well." Mercy sent a fond glance toward the slumbering girls. "I pray they adjust quickly."

"And what about you, Mercy Feathers? Will you adjust quickly?"

His voice had dropped to a low, husky, and wickedly seductive tenor.

"*Me?*" she all but squeaked.

"Aye. You." A smile teased one side of his mouth in that rakish manner that made her feel all squishy inside. "Everyone's attention and concern has focused on Bellamy and Arabelle. But your life has been turned teakettle over spout too."

She almost believed he cared.

Mercy's tummy quivered. Something foreign and warm pooled in her center while something else entirely tingled behind her breastbone.

Lord, what was wrong with her?

Of a sudden, she was much too warm.

Had the room suddenly shrunk?

Had Ronan moved closer?

He surely seemed as if he had. His masculine presence dominated the area until all Mercy could see, hear, and sense was him. The tempting heat of his body, the aromas of sandalwood, mint, and that woodsy essence that always seemed to emanate from him beckoned her. And tonight, there was also the faint odor of spirits.

Brandy? Whisky?

Her traitorous body swayed toward his, much like gravity pulled objects to the earth. They had no choice any more than she did at this moment.

"My concern is for the girls. Their happiness." Stiffening her spine, she attempted to put a bit of starch in her tone and feared she'd failed dismally. "As you well know, my lord, servants do as they are bid. Go where they are told."

If they wanted to keep their posts, that was.

"Ah, but I would have you happy as well, Mercy." He touched a calloused fingertip to her jaw. "Tell me. What would make *you* happy?"

At Ronan's brazen but soft touch, a bolt of sensation jolted through Mercy, causing her heart to beat a jagged rhythm as if she'd been electrocuted. Could a person erupt into flames from a mere touch?

He trailed that long finger along her jawbone, and she shuddered.

From the roguish smile arching his mouth, he'd felt her shiver and took it for what it was.

Scorching desire.

Yes, indeed. Mercy was in danger of incinerating. All that would be left was a pile of cinders where she'd once stood.

For one deliciously appalling moment, she thought Ronan was going to kiss her. Right there in the nursery with the girls mere feet away.

What was more, Mercy wanted him to. Her mind

shouted "No, it's wrong. It's wicked and sinful."

But her heart and body urged her to disregard wisdom and morality.

This was utter madness.

Clearing her throat, she stepped away. She sent the girls another sidelong glance, assuring herself they slept on, oblivious to the sensual sparks exploding but a few feet away.

Ronan played a dangerous game, and she didn't intend to be the loser. Governesses, maids, abigails, nurses, cooks, companions... Female servants were always the losers in this sort of contest. By all that was holy, Mercy would not be counted among those feather-headed goosecaps.

"My contentment is dependent upon your wards' happiness. I love them and would see them adapt to their new lives with alacrity and ease." That wasn't even an attempt to be subtle as she reminded him of both of their positions. "I should think that would be your first priority too."

That accusation was impudent and unfair, and Mercy knew it.

"*Touché*, Quiritis."

She puzzled her brow. "Quiritis?"

What in the world was he on about now?

"Aye, the Roman goddess of motherhood. You love my wards as much as any mother would or could." Out of habit, he grazed two fingers along his scar. "I am grateful, and I'm sure they are too."

Emotion throttled up Mercy's throat and lodged

there like a cannonball—huge and heavy.

Was he testing her again?

To see if she were qualified to teach the girls?

A thread of pride straightened her spine. Mercy knew her deity history. Quiritis was the Sabine *pre*-Roman goddess of motherhood.

She swallowed before saying crisply, "Latona *is* the Roman goddess of motherhood." For good measure, she added, "And Leto is the Greek Titan goddess of motherhood, but so is Rhea."

A rather devilish grin lit his brown eyes, darkened to the color of melted chocolate.

She felt as if she were melting in their depths.

"Ah, but Rhea is also the goddess of fertility," he said with that sideways grin that did impossible things to her pulse.

An outraged gasp tried to pass her lips, but she meshed them together.

Too far.

That was too far.

Mercy refused to allow her mind to wander that treacherous path. Ronan Brockman murmuring the word fertility in that rumbling purr might very well be the most evocative thing she'd ever heard.

It was time to leave before things heated up any further. Before Mercy said or did something imprudent that she'd later regret.

"I shall bid you good evening, my lord." She angled toward the door. Hopefully, her bath awaited her, but she wasn't saying a word about it to him.

Tomorrow perhaps she would thank him properly for his consideration in ordering a bath for her. Tonight, mentioning a bath would only lead to thoughts of being naked.

No, indeed.

Mercy wasn't going to do something so profoundly ill-advised and provocative in front of him.

"Running away?" Ronan softly taunted.

Mercy froze for half a second, one hand on the latch, before tearing from the chamber as if hell's hoary hounds nipped her heels.

Yes. I am running away.

His rich laugh teased her ears until she closed her chamber door.

After turning the key in the lock, Mercy leaned against the panel, hands braced on either side of her hips. Chest rising and falling with adrenaline sweeping through her, she bit the inside corner of her mouth.

How could she go from loathing him one minute to melting from his touch the next?

She wasn't a promiscuous miss. She was a moral woman.

What just happened in the nursery must never transpire again.

Muffled footfalls echoed in the corridor, and she held her breath as they stopped directly outside her chamber door.

"Good night, Mercy. Sweet dreams."

Allowing her eyelids to flutter closed, she whispered, "Lord, what am I going to do?"

*She will receive the best of care, as do all
of the girls who make Haven House and
Academy for the Enrichment of Young Women
their home. Rest assured, the child will be loved,
educated, and raised to be a poised, confident, and
accomplished young woman, capable of making
her own way in the world. I pride myself on my
unwavering discretion and surreptitiousness. Not
a single one of my charges' true identities has
ever become known. Your privacy is assured.*

~ Mrs. Hester Shepherd in a letter to
Mercy Feathers's benefactor

13

*Bond Street, London
A fortnight later*

Why, by all of the divine powers, had Ronan
agreed to this outing?

Barely refraining from rolling his eyes and turning
on his heel, he nodded a greeting to a pair of ladies
wearing godawful bonnets and held the door open for
them as they entered *Le Belle Haute Couture* before
him. Whispering and looking over their shoulders to
where he stood, they swept inside the decidedly frilly

feminine establishment.

He was fairly certain he didn't know either woman. If he did, their names escaped him, and he didn't give ten figs that they had. He'd never been one to care a whit about who was or was not in town. Nor did he note which females were new to the Marriage Mart each Season or which spinsters and wallflowers returned year after year, ever more wilted and disheartened.

As a younger son, he'd been blessedly spared the hassle, obligation, and pressure of marrying and producing an heir. Until inheriting the guardianship, Ronan's life had been unfettered and unencumbered. He'd been free to pursue his interests and indulge his hobbies, both in England and abroad.

Something, truth be told, he still hankered to do.

One couldn't very well tow two round-eyed innocents to a boxing match, a horserace, or to inspect the latest cargo from India or other Oriental ports.

Could one?

And yet here he was, at exactly half of two as his mother had ordered, standing deucedly out of place outside a modiste's shop and acting the part of a doting parent, so to speak.

Attempting to erase the pained expression from his face, for he supposed he had a good decade of this type of torture before him, he glanced up and down the street. At least fate hadn't conspired to have anyone he knew spy him entering the establishment.

He was good and done with the jests, disparaging remarks, and poking fun at his expense.

Even Ronan's more sensible friends, Landry Audsley, Earl of Keyworth, Allen Wimpleton, and Kingston Barclay, had quirked skeptical brows while grinning like bosky sailors over their glasses of brandy. Ewan McTavish, Viscount Sethwick, whose wife owned Stapleton Shipping and Supplies and with whom Ronan had a business relationship, had dissolved into laughter that he poorly disguised as a coughing fit.

God rot them.

Worst of all, Ronan's closest friend Jason Steele, the captain of *The Arcturus,* had laughed so hard he'd upset his glass of whisky by pounding his fist upon the table.

"*You*, Brockman? A guardian to *girls*?" Jason chortled while wiping his eyes. "Masterson must've been good and desperate."

Bloody American sod.

Well, half American. Steele's maternal grandfather was a British earl, though he'd never met the man.

"Laugh all you want, Steele. My guardianship may well mean I will have to entrust you with my responsibilities in America."

At once, Jason sobered. "You know you can count on me, Ronan. Whatever you need."

"I know." It relieved Ronan's mind a great deal.

He need never leave England again if he didn't wish to.

Did he wish to?

Yes, of course.

What about his wards?

Blast his indecisiveness.

Venting his ire, Ronan kicked viciously at a pebble.

Why everyone thought it so absurdly hilarious that *he* should be named a guardian had become downright insulting and offensive. There was nothing in his past or his character to warrant such mockery—at least not to his way of thinking.

This guardianship business—if done correctly, as he was determined to do—was a pain in the... His attention fell on the rock he'd just kicked.

Well, a blasted pebble in one's shoe. A sharp, pointy stone that aggravated incessantly.

The shop door made a loud *snick* when he shoved it shut with perhaps a tad more force than necessary.

Having wards took a bit of getting accustomed to, that was all.

In time, he would get the hang of it.

Wouldn't he?

Naturally, to do the thing right meant spending time with Arabelle and Bellamy. Which, often—far too often for his raging libido—meant spending time with their much too attractive governess as well.

A governess who, since he'd held her in his arms

in Masterson's study, had managed to wheedle her way into his thoughts far more frequently than Ronan liked. Most assuredly, far more often than was appropriate.

He could still remember the sensation of her lush feminine form in his arms as she wept. The tantalizing softness and tempting warmth. Her slightly spicy fragrance—cloves, perhaps—and the texture of her silky hair, which smelled of spring and wildflowers, against his cheek.

Regardless, Mercy had all but given him the frozen shoulder since the night in the nursery. Oh, she remained impeccably polite, but no smiles were sent his way. No curious looks from her spectacular green eyes. No swiftly tossed glares or eyes softening with approval.

Ronan would even take her rancor and dislike over this cool-as-a-cucumber, aloof civility. He hadn't even kissed her as he'd yearned to do and felt like quite the chivalrous gentleman for abstaining. She'd likely have slapped his face, or at the very least, rang him a peal if she had any notion just how much restraint he'd dredged up the other night.

His powerful attraction to Mercy also scared the hair off his head. He'd be as bald as Mother's three brothers—bare as eggs, the lot—if he didn't get his ardor under control.

Ronan knew his fascination with Mercy was inappropriate. Unlike many of the upper ten thousand, Brockman men did not chase after servants. To do so was an abuse of their power and position.

One has a responsibility to respect and protect one's employees. To be an example and, above all, to act honorably toward them at all times.

Hadn't he heard that mantra from first his grandfather and then his father too many times to count? Sanford was also wont to raise an imperial brow and rattle off the same diatribe.

Besides, his parents—Sanford too, for that matter—would be appalled. The Trentholms might be more forward-thinking than a significant number of their peers. Nonetheless, leopards belonged with leopards, zebras with zebras, flamingos with flamingos, and so on and so on.

Never in the history of the illustrious Brockman lineage had a single Brockman married outside of their social class.

Marriage?

No, Ronan wasn't considering marrying Mercy.

But Benjamin?

A private grin edged Ronan's mouth upward.

Aye, Ben's little secret might not be a secret much longer. The scandal would be deliciously monumental. In point of fact, Ronan would finagle a way to be present when Sanford learned of the entanglement. That ought to provide enough entertainment to last for a month, at the very least.

While the marquess and marchioness of Trentholm were loving and supportive, aristocrats and commoners were from two utterly different and incompatible worlds in their superior minds.

It was wrong to lust after Mercy.

Ronan knew that.

The problem was, Ronan's healthy male body didn't quite agree. When he'd requested his fourth cold bath last week, Sturges had given him a decidedly peculiar look. As if he wasn't sure if Ronan was in his right mind.

His bloody mind was perfectly fine. It was the rest of him that was aflame.

"It's something I picked up in America," Ronan fabricated last evening when making another request for cold bathwater. "Great for the constitution—very rejuvenating. Prevents illness, increases my energy, and even helps me sleep."

Ronan had no idea if any of that manufactured twaddle was true, but Sturges appeared suitably convinced and impressed.

"Helps one sleep, you say?" the butler mused, his gaze aglow with keen interest. "Mrs. Sturges suffers from frequent insomnia, which regrettably, keeps me awake too."

He suddenly smiled widely. The occurrence was so rare that Ronan blinked twice. Sturges' resemblance to a grinning hound was quite extraordinary. And most disturbing in a macabre way.

"I'll suggest she take a cold bath tonight," Sturges said, his eyes alight with anticipation.

Poor Mrs. Sturges. Pray to God, she could forgive Ronan, and there'd be no irreparable harm to the Sturges' decades-old marriage.

Once inside the fashionable shop, Ronan blinked, taking a moment for his eyes to adjust to the interior.

Neat bolts of fabric of every imaginable color and texture were exhibited along the far wall according to hue. Another wall held ribbons, lace, braiding, and all sorts of other haberdashery items. A long black velvet curtain blocked the view to the back of the shop where he presumed fittings took place.

A counter displaying a variety of other wares occupied the fourth wall. Throughout the shop, bonnets, fallalls, fripperies, and other accoutrements were shown to their best advantage on tables and hat stands. A particularly garish pink and olive-green bonnet with a froth of flowers and feathers snagged Ronan's attention.

The thing was positively hideous.

What woman would put that millinery atrocity on her head?

Even as Ronan regarded the offense to the eye, the pair he'd held the door open for made a beeline for the travesty and began gushing over it.

Well, that answered that question.

He glanced to the window.

Unseasonably warm, the sun blazed outdoors today.

Dratted, annoying orb.

March, known for her heavy rain, heavier fog, and permeating dankness, had decided to cast off her shroud of gloom and burst forth under the guise of a late August afternoon.

Which was why he'd been cajoled into meeting his mother, sisters, and wards at the dressmaker's to escort them to Gunter's. Rather, he'd received a note from his mother informing him that he was to do so at precisely half of two.

Evidently, she believed he'd neglected his wards this past week. Which, of course, was utter balderdash. A mere three days had passed since he'd escorted them to Hyde Park to feed the ducks and fly kites.

Couldn't a man take a day for himself for manly pursuits?

Weren't there enough females around to keep the girls company?

Just last week, Mother had hosted a tea and there had been at least six girls near in age to Bellamy and Arabelle. He knew, for a fact, that they'd received three reciprocal invitations as a result.

Regardless, Arabelle and Bellamy had never tasted an ice, and today's weather called for such an indulgence. He didn't begrudge them the experience, one he'd enjoyed often as a child. What he did begrudge was having to climb inside an infernally hot coach.

Unless…

He perked up.

Perhaps Mother had thought to bring the landau. With the top lowered, that might be tolerable.

His enthusiasm evaporated just as rapidly.

Who was he kidding?

The women had parasols to help block the sun. He had a bloody black hat perched atop his head, acting as a heat magnet. The sun would beat down upon him—unrelenting and remorseless.

Gunter's would be a bevy of activity in this weather too. Best to get on with it, for the brutal heat would only increase as the afternoon advanced. March had no business pretending to be a summer month, thereby throwing everything off-kilter.

Ronan strode forward, conscious of the eyes upon him.

The lone male, he stood out like a peacock among pigeons.

Several women turned to take his measure, including Mercy. A shadow of disquiet flashed across her face and then was gone.

Of course, she was here.

His mother wouldn't dream of leaving Mercy home to do whatever governesses did when their charges were elsewhere.

What, exactly, *did* they do?

Nap? Read? Take a walk? Write a letter?

At once, Mercy turned a delightful shade of pink, almost an exact match to the bolt of fabric she held and to which Bellamy—still wearing mourning black—gazed longingly.

Mother insisted Bellamy and Arabelle might be permitted to wear a bit of color. Nothing too outrageous yet. A dark blue or violet. Assuredly not the pale petal pink Bellamy stared at with heart-wrenching yearning.

However, Ronan was their guardian. If *he* wanted to purchase colorful frocks for his wards, then who was to stop him? He didn't give ten curses what *le beau monde* thought of the girls wearing colors so early after their father's passing.

If a pretty gown cheered them up, then so be it. Lovely frocks that dripped with ruffles and bows and buttons and lace, if they so desired. Ronan would speak with Mademoiselle De la Cour himself regarding the matter.

Would a dozen for each of his wards suffice? Naturally, with matching slippers and any other fripperies necessary.

Mercy would know what was needed.

He'd ask her. It would give him just the excuse Ronan desired to have a few moments alone with her without his conscience chiding him like the flames of hell licking at his heels.

You are a bounder and a churl, Ronan Mitchell Forsythe Brockman.

So much for his over-zealous conscience keeping silent.

Devil take scruples and integrity.

It is the oddest thing. Lady Corinna acted as if
She recognized me. She mentioned a duke too,
but Lady Trentholm cut her off before she said
his name. So far, there has been no discussion
of terminating my position. Nonetheless,
I cannot squelch my growing unease.
The Brockmans know something they
aren't telling me. I'm sure of it.
Do you suppose I should write
Mrs. Shepherd? Would she be
Forthright with me? Can she be?

~ Miss Mercy Feathers in a letter to
Miss Purity Mayfield

Le Belle Haute Couture
Bond Street

Quite pleased with his decision, Ronan strode across the wooden floor to do just that. "Bellamy, do you like that color?"

"Oh, yes," she breathed and nodded. "Pink is my favorite color. Then green, lavender, red, and blue," she elucidated in quick succession. Wrinkling her nose, she said, "I quite dislike brown, orange, and gray." Giving her gown a rueful glance, she added, "And black."

What little girl didn't?

"Lord Ronan?" Arabelle, who'd been silent up to this point, bounced on her toes and tugged at his sleeve.

Something unfurled behind his breastbone at her trusting gesture. "Yes, Arabelle?"

"I adore yellow like sunflowers and blue like robin eggs. And the color of the ocean too." She plucked at her skirt. "Not this awful black like all of the joy has been sucked from the fabric."

He couldn't argue with her assessment.

"My favorite color is green," Ronan volunteered. *Fern green, to be precise.* Much like a pretty governess's eyes. "What's yours, Miss Feathers?"

The startled look Mercy speared him before narrowing her eyes all but shouted, "I know what you are up to, and I'm not having a bit of it."

Bellamy puzzled her forehead. "What *is* your favorite color, Miss Mercy? You always wear the same gray, dark blue, or dull brown."

"It's dark red." A rosy hue tinged Mercy's cheeks.
Well, I'll be buggered.

Ronan would also vow she didn't own a single red article of clothing.

Red was a scandalous shade to favor. And yet, it was perfect for this woman with streaks of fire in her hair and embers smoldering beneath her modulated decorum.

Corrina and Marissa appeared from behind the

curtain, which was a most excellent thing. Because as his wayward mind had of late, it trundled straight down a wicked path to imagining Mercy in a filmy crimson nightgown.

For certain, he would burn in hell.

"Ronan," Corinna said with a welcoming grin. "I cannot wait for ices. I thought I would melt during my fitting. Was there ever such a warm March day before? And to think, just two years ago, we didn't have a summer at all to speak of."

Ronan glanced at his wards, their little faces animated as they took in the bolts and bolts of bright cloth.

"Have my wards' measurements been taken?"

"Last week, Ronan," Marissa offered with a pretty smile as she took the girls' hands. "Come, dears. You must see the selection of reticules, fichus, and fans that just arrived from Paris. There are small ones, just your size."

"May we, Miss Mercy?" Arabelle asked.

A wave of pride swelled within Ronan. They were well-behaved little girls. He knew who was responsible for that.

"Of course." Angling her head, Mercy smiled. "Be sure to stay with Lady Marissa though, and don't touch."

Nodding eagerly, they bustled away.

"Mother should be along shortly. Mademoiselle De la Cour was just finishing pinning Mama's morning gown," Corinna said helpfully.

"Corrina, dearest!"

The three of them turned as Cathryn Knighton, a statuesque brunette, sailed into the boutique accompanied by an older, stern-faced maid.

"Cathryn!" Corinna exclaimed with equal exuberance. "I didn't know you had come up to town already."

Corinna rushed to embrace her friend.

Laughing, Miss Knighton hugged Corinna. "Henry had some sort of business to see to. Naturally, I insisted I be allowed to accompany him. It's never too soon to have new gowns commissioned for the Season."

Ronan thought the maid might've muttered something ungracious beneath her breath which sounded decidedly like, "As if you need any more," before cinching her mouth shut.

In all the years he had known the dervish that was Cathryn Knighton—at least fifteen, wasn't it?—he'd never once seen her wear the same frock twice. Henry had his hands full with his sister.

Looping her arm through Miss Knighton's, Corinna returned to Ronan's side.

He didn't miss Mercy retreating a few steps.

He despised the subservient mien she'd adopted. However, it wasn't any different than that of Cathryn's chaperone or the other three or four maids attempting to make themselves invisible within the shop.

Wasn't that the way of it?

Servants were expected to be at the ready but always unobtrusive.

"Ronan, you know Cathryn," Corinna said, still smiling widely.

His sister and Cathryn Knighton were two peas in a pod. Both enjoyed thumbing their noses at society's strictures.

Dipping his head, Ronan murmured, "It's always a pleasure, Miss Knighton."

"I understand you've acquired wards since I last saw you?" Mischief sparkled in her light brandy-brown eyes, and Cathryn grinned. Nothing the least subtle about this hellion.

"Indeed," he said.

Corinna had been busy, it seemed. He leveled her a chastising glance, but she just lifted a shoulder. Such juicy news couldn't be contained, he knew. And Miss Knighton was her dearest friend.

Of its own accord, his gaze traveled across the shop to where Bellamy and Arabelle admired a child-sized cobalt blue and silver mantle. He made a mental note to purchase it and another in lavender when he returned to order the girls' gowns.

"Is that them?" Miss Knighton asked, pointing her attention toward the trio now *oohing* and *aahing* over a child-size brisé fan.

"It is," he answered shortly.

"They are positively adorable," Cathryn said.

"Jenine will arrive in a fortnight. We shall have to have them to tea. I'm sure they'd get along famously with Bridgette and Matilda." She pulled a face. "Not the boys, though. Robert and Edward are simply little terrors. Exact replicas of Henry at that age."

Henry Knighton, now the Earl of Towler, had attended university with Ronan. He'd been two years ahead and had married Jenine shortly thereafter.

Mercy set the bolt atop the nearby table and made to slip past them. "Please excuse me. I really shouldn't leave Lady Marissa to mind the girls for long."

That drew everyone's attention to her.

"Forgive me, Miss Feathers," Corinna apologized. "Cathryn, this is Miss Mercy Feathers, the girls' governess. Miss Feathers, Lady Cathryn Knighton, sister to the Earl of Towler."

Mercy dipped a shallow curtsy. "My lady."

"Good heavens!" Miss Knighton gasped, her eyes widening comically. "How is it possible?"

She slid Corinna a dumbfounded look.

"Not now, Cathryn," Corinna chided, dragging her friend away.

"But…" Miss Knighton protested, still gaping at Mercy's pale-as-milk face.

"Shh." Corinna shushed her, still towing her by the elbow. "It's uncanny. *I know.*"

She stopped a few feet away and whispered furiously to her friend, who nodded, though her rapt attention continued to slide to Mercy every few seconds.

Mercy turned her confused gaze to Ronan.

"I *don't* know," he said honestly.

And he didn't.

Nevertheless, he meant to get to the bottom of whatever *this* was. His mother had been remarkably closed mouth about Corinna's outburst two weeks ago. He'd approached her regarding the matter thrice, and she'd neatly turned the conversation to avoid answering him.

Now Miss Knighton acted as if she'd seen a ghost. *Good God.*

What if others reacted in the same manner?

Had others responded the same way?

Ronan had absolutely no idea how many outings Mercy had accompanied his mother on or if she'd been introduced to any callers.

Even as the thought entered his mind, his stepmother, looking somewhat piqued, emerged from behind the draperies, Mademoiselle *tutting* comfortingly behind her.

"Zee headache has afflicted Madame," she offered in an imperfect French accent.

Mademoiselle De la Cour was as French as Ronan was Arabian, or the Prince Regent was a Corinthian or monogamous.

"Ronan, I fear I've developed the most dreadful megrim," Mother said apologetically, the pinched look around her eyes and mouth revealing how much she suffered. "An outing to Gunter's is out of the question." *Praise God.* "And I even thought to use the landau so we might enjoy the weather," she lamented.

"My lady, I would be happy to offer the use of my carriage," Miss Knighton offered with genuine concern. "That way, you will be spared the sun's glare, and Lord Ronan may take his charges for their promised ices."

Evidently, upon seeing Mother, Corinna had deemed it safe to return with her not-so-subtle friend. By that time, Marissa and the girls had also joined them, and the discussion Miss Knighton had been so eager to initiate must wait.

"We're not going to have ices?" Arabelle asked, her disappointment tangible.

Mercy stepped to her side, careful to keep her face averted from Miss Knighton.

She shouldn't be ashamed, especially since neither Ronan nor she had any idea what Miss Knighton's exclamation meant. Or what Corinna's had, for that matter.

"I'm sorry," Mercy said, sinking onto her haunches before Arabelle. She took both of the little girl's hands in hers and gave a gentle squeeze. "But we will have to visit Gunter's another day."

"Not a bit of it," Mother corrected, though she winced when she spoke. She indeed was miserable. "I shall gladly accept your offer, Miss Knighton."

"I shall as well," Corinna put in with a sideways glance toward Mercy. "We've simply heaps to catch up on, Cathryn."

"Well, it's settled then," Ronan said, somewhat mollified. Five stuffed into a carriage was loads better than seven.

Not five minutes later, he sat in the landau, his back to the driver. Rather than sitting beside him, Marissa had taken the seat between Arabelle and Bellamy. That meant Mercy was obliged to sit beside him.

He didn't believe his youngest sister was matchmaking. Since the girls arrived, Marissa had treated them like adored younger sisters. They obviously felt the same way and sought out her company whenever possible.

Mercy spoke not a word as the coachman maneuvered the conveyance through the thronging street toward Berkeley Square. Facing slightly away from the occupants, she stared out the vehicle.

Ronan didn't miss the slight furrowing of her brow or the occasional tightening of her lips. He'd wager his new shipping investment in *The Arcturus* that she was pondering Cathryn Knighton's outburst and Corinna's alacrity in hushing her friend. Probably Mother's too.

He loathed the uncertainty and confusion that flashed in Mercy's eyes, but he positively despised the glimmer of fear there as well.

What did she have to be afraid of?

"Lord Ronan?"

He turned his head at Arabelle's inquiry.

"May Miss Mercy have an ice too? Please?"

Mercy jerked her head toward Arabelle. "Darling, that's not necessary."

"But you've never tasted an ice either, Miss Mercy," Bellamy protested.

"Never? Truly?" Marissa asked, her eyes owlish with astonishment. No doubt she, who'd lived a cosseted, privileged life, couldn't fathom going without anything. "Not a sorbet or cream ice either?"

A small smile drew Mercy's mouth upward. "I'm not aware of any establishment that serves ices, cream ices, or sorbets in Rochester."

Or Essex, he'd vow.

What Father had shared about Haven House and Academy for the Enrichment of Young Women this morning had proved most intriguing.

Most intriguing, indeed.

I am sure you can understand the delicacy
of the situation. My patrons entrust me
with anonymity and absolute discretion.
I have given my word not to divulge their
identities, and as a Christian, I am honor-bound
before the good Lord to keep that vow. My wards
are not even aware of who their parents are. I regret
I cannot be of further service regarding your inquiry.

~ Mrs. Hester Shepherd in a letter to Lord Trentholm

15

Gunter's Tea Shop
Berkeley Square
An hour later

Almost sighing with delight, Mercy dabbed her mouth with her handkerchief. The lemon sorbet had been heavenly, particularly refreshing given the afternoon's warmth. Despite her oath to herself to maintain a respectful, professional distance from Ronan, she couldn't help but offer him a grateful smile.

"That was the most delicious thing I've ever tasted," she said, setting aside her dish and spoon for a waiter to collect.

"I confess, I could easily eat two or three," Ronan said with a self-deprecating chuckle. "We are most fortunate our French chef has several recipes for ices, cream ice, sorbets, and bombs. He indulges the family at least once a month."

She laughed, quite pleased by that news. "The girls will be delighted, I'm sure."

"You too, I should think." Ronan winked, then wriggled his eyebrows playfully. "Escoffier always makes sure there is plenty." He patted his hard, flat stomach. "We Brockmans all have sweet tooths."

On the pretense of keeping an eye upon her charges, Mercy swept a covert glance around them.

He shouldn't wink at her. Someone might see and jump to the wrong conclusion. Take the gesture for more than an employer's teasing.

The tea shop overflowed with overheated patrons eager to sample the sweets. At Ronan's suggestion, Mercy and the others had opted to eat inside the landau conveniently parked beneath a cluster of stately oaks' welcoming shade.

It was cooler outside than in the overcrowded shop anyway.

Unlike Bellamy and Arabelle, who'd gobbled their chocolate cream ices like starving urchins and now wandered nearby with Marissa, laughing at squirrels and chattering with other children, Mercy had relished every scrumptious bite.

Such a rare treat was to be savored.

Ronan had chosen burnt filbert cream ice, which had disappeared with nearly the swiftness of the girls' treats. He still sat beside her in the landau, and she sent another surreptitious glance around them to see if anyone had noted the unusual arrangement.

Perhaps she ought to move to the vehicle's other side. But that might cause even more speculation. In truth, no matter what she did, if a chinwag wanted to find something to gossip about, they would find a morsel.

A governess ought not to be quite so friendly with her employer. It led to undesirable speculation.

Her perusal revealed no one seemed to be paying them any particular mind, and she relaxed a trifle.

One arm thrown across the back of the seat, Ronan angled toward her until their knees touched. He seemed not to notice, but Mercy discreetly drew away.

"I intend to purchase gowns for each of the girls in colors more befitting children," he said. "Since Mademoiselle De la Cour has already taken their measurements, I had hoped you would assist me in selecting fabrics and all of the other necessities a young girl requires."

"But my lord, your mother has already commissioned several gowns for them."

She hadn't expected he'd be such a generous man. Truth be told, she still didn't know if he was magnanimous with his own monies or his fathers. Not that it was any of her business. Except...one

180

exemplified a considerate, caring, kindhearted man and the other a privileged opportunist.

"I'm aware, Mercy, but being mindful of their mourning period, Mother probably selected somber shades, didn't she?" He crossed his legs, drawing her attention to their buff-colored masculine length.

Averting her gaze—moral young women did not stare at men's rippling thigh muscles—Mercy said, "She did. It's appropriate for mourning. You needn't go to further expense."

His derisive snort startled her, and she barely resisted peering around to see who had noticed. Hopefully, no one had.

"Miss Feathers, I assure you, I can well afford to clothe my wards. They will never go without anything while under my care."

That answered the question about his funds.

"Bellamy and Arabelle are my responsibility," Ronan went on. "It's only because I don't wish to offend my parents that I permit them the indulgence of making purchases on behalf of the girls."

"I understand." Another piece of Mercy's heart dropped at his feet. Ronan was truly one of the most thoughtful people she'd ever met.

Gazing at them laughing with a group of children several feet away, a fond smile bent his mouth. "I would have them wear bright colors that prompt memories of happier things rather than have their attire constantly remind them of their loss."

She brought her gaze up to meet his, unable to hide her appreciation.

"I think it a splendid idea, Ronan. I've never held with forcing children to grieve for a full year. They need to move on. It's much healthier, I think."

"In that, we are of one mind," Ronan murmured, gazing into her eyes in such a profound way that it was as if he stared into her very soul. Very deep within her, something clicked. She wasn't sure if something had been released or locked. Nevertheless, whatever it was, she felt oddly emotional and moved.

To cover her confusion and awareness of him as a male rather than her employer, Mercy let her gaze linger on Arabelle and Bellamy.

"The girls are doing much better than I had dared to hope." Feeling a bit chagrined, she peeked up at him through her lashes. "I confess, being their guardian suits you."

Ronan quirked his mouth into a wholly masculine smile. "From you, Mercy, that is high praise indeed."

The heat of a flush climbed her neck and cheeks. Having no fan, she waved her hand before her face. "My, but it is warm for March."

"I think this weather is just a tease," Ronan said, removing his hat and sweeping his hand over his glossy hair before replacing it. "Likely, in a week, the rains will come once more, and we'll be drenched until April."

He dipped his strong chin in greeting toward a

passing couple when the man doffed his hat. The haughty lady swiftly veered her attention from Ronan's scarred face. Her focus landed on Mercy, and her eyes narrowed, then narrowed further.

The gentleman at her side, attired in the first stare of fashion, peered disconcertingly at Mercy before bending his neck to hear something the stylish woman on his arm whispered frantically into his ear while gesturing wildly.

A tiny crease appeared between Ronan's eyebrows before he returned his regard to Mercy.

"Mercy, forgive my prying. You said you were orphaned, but clearly you bear a marked resemblance to someone given my sister's, mother's, and Miss Knighton's reaction."

"I suspect the lady and gentleman who just passed by as well," she murmured, sounding rather doleful. Her shoulders lifted as she inhaled deeply, then blew the breath out with a little puff of her lips.

"I do not know what it means," she said honestly. "Perhaps they've mistaken me for someone else? I can tell you with certainty that I do not know if either of my parents are alive. I spent my childhood in an orphanage."

That wasn't all Haven House and Academy for the Enrichment of Young Women was, but the description was apt if not complete.

"I know Haven House and Academy for the Enrichment of Young Women is where you were raised and received an education," he said kindly.

Instantly on her guard at the abrupt change of subject, she stiffened and drew back. "How, precisely, did you come by that information?"

"Your letter of recommendation was among Lieutenant Masterson's papers."

"Oh. Of course. How silly of me." That made sense. Prepared for a battle, Mercy felt somewhat deflated. But in a good way. For heaven's sake, she mustn't act defensive, or that would raise Ronan's suspicions.

Wait a moment.

That recommendation hadn't included any information about Mercy's childhood.

How did Ronan know she'd been raised there?

Dread slithered along her shoulders, cold and clammy.

Checking to see that the girls were still engaged elsewhere, she clasped her hands together atop her lap. The sorbet curdled in her stomach as she comprehended exactly what he was saying.

Ronan had been checking up on her.

He'd find nothing. Hester Shepherd was paid very well to ensure that.

"There was nothing in my letter of recommendation that mentioned where I was raised, your lordship."

He gave her a sheepish grin, the movement pulling his scar slightly. She'd become so accustomed to the puckered flesh, she hardly noticed it any longer. For certain, Mercy didn't believe it detracted from his good looks. What was more, he didn't appear self-conscious or ashamed of it.

It was a war wound, after all.

Weren't men boastful about such things?

"I had my father look into the establishment," he admitted in that straightforward manner that both pleased and peeved.

I had my father look into the establishment.

Mercy digested that bit of information. Anger wrestled with reason. Ronan had a right to know the background of the governess charged with educating his wards. On the other hand, she couldn't help but feel his prying was something more.

"Why?" she asked bluntly.

"I should think it obvious," he returned a trifle less amiable than the charming rogue of but seconds before. "I wanted to know as much as I can about the woman acting as my wards' governess." His expression hardened the merest bit, and the earlier twinkle in his eye was nowhere to be found. "I cannot think why you would object if you've nothing to hide."

Was he accusing her again?

That rankled, causing her ire to rise, swift and intense.

Mercy had not yet forgiven him for practically calling her a whore and a liar. Was he also insinuating she had an insidious past? She'd wager her cross brooch *his* past was less saintly than hers.

If Ronan knew she was a bastard, would he dismiss her? Without reference?

Mercy's indignation evaporated as a wave of fear, sharp and icy, buffeted her. Panic sprouted, capering along her veins.

Mrs. Shepherd wouldn't reveal that truth. Surely she would not, for she knew what the repercussions would be to all of her current and former students, not to mention her own livelihood. The students' true origins at Haven House and Academy for the Enrichment of Young Women always remained ambiguous.

Clenching her hands, Mercy thrust her chin up. "I have nothing to be ashamed of."

That was true. She had nothing whatsoever to do with the origins of her birth.

She couldn't, however, vow that she had nothing to hide because she did.

Nevertheless, she would not be chagrined about her parentage. Mrs. Shepherd had insisted upon that. She made it clear from the moment her students were old enough to comprehend that they were not defective or flawed or responsible. They were victims of other peoples' rash, imprudent, and unkind choices.

Regardless, they would not live their lives acting the victims. Feeling sorry for themselves, wallowing in self-pity, always blaming someone else for their situation, and never taking ownership of their own lives and circumstances.

That, Mrs. Shepherd said, was how the cowardly behaved. Her girls were intrepid and strong and courageous.

"Life is what you make of it, my dears. Give thanks in all circumstances," Mrs. Shepherd had said. Which, in truth, was much easier to say than to actually have to put into practice.

"But you're not really an orphan, are you?" Ronan uncrossed his legs and leaned nearer. "None of the girls raised at Haven House and Academy for the Enrichment of Young Women are, are they?"

Mercy felt the blood drain from her face and curled her toes into her boots until they cramped.

Why was he doing this?

If Ronan already had the answers, why torment her?

Dampening her lower lip with her tongue, and absently noticing he followed the movement with his avid gaze, she drew in a fortifying breath. Just as he had in the study, he was testing her. She was certain of it.

"I sincerely do not know whether I am or not." That was true. Her parents might both very well be dead. *And they might also be alive.* "How does that have any bearing upon my qualifications or performance of my duties?"

Ronan shrugged casually and relaxed back into the squabs once more.

"I never said it did, Mercy. I honestly don't care two farthings if you are illegitimate."

At her slight gasp and furtive glance around, he frowned. He also swept his gaze about them.

"Forgive me," he said in a more subdued tone. "That was not well done of me. It was insensitive and tactless."

"The truth often is, my lord," she snapped, her stiff form attesting to her humiliation and offense. She didn't care if he knew the truth. Nevertheless, he'd never have spoken to a lady as he just had to her, which was a testament to how little he regarded her.

Why had Ronan chosen this public place for such a private conversation? It incensed and frustrated her to think he'd manipulated what was supposed to be a special outing to suit his agenda.

Thrumming his fingertips on the edge of the landau, he said, "What I do care about is how it will affect my wards."

Not well, of course. Ronan knew the intricacies of *le beau monde*'s snobbery.

Society seldom allowed grace or clemency for the under orders but excused themselves all manner of offenses, including shunting unwanted by-blows into obscurity.

Accused, tried, and convicted all because of something Mercy had no control over. How did those born on the wrong side of the blanket differ in character, integrity, and honor from those with the advantage of their sire's surname?

"So those of us without the benefit of parents sanctified by marriage vows are not permitted to hold respectable positions? Our parents' sins must cast a shadow of shame upon us and smudge our reputations, making us less deserving?" Less worthy?" She gave him a reproving look. "That is rather archaic, don't you think?"

"Aye, it is," Ronan admitted with a half-nod.

A dribble of perspiration trickled down his face and over his scar, and he swiped it away. He must be miserably warm in his coat. Mercy only wore a light muslin shawl over her gown, and it had long since slid to the seat. Her plain straw bonnet provided shade from the sun without the added warmth of her black bonnet.

Stop it. Ronan Brockman doesn't merit your empathy.

"But, Mercy, that doesn't change the fact that we live in a culture where such ill-fated truths have long-reaching and irreparable consequences. I'm not saying that it's right or that I even agree. I'm just stating the facts. I need to know what I'm up against in order to keep Arabelle and Bellamy safe. You too, for that matter."

That last bit took her aback.

Me too?

He was right, of course.

Mercy was as impressed with Ronan's logic as she

was vexed with the irrefutable facts he so calmly presented. He would've done well in Parliament, given his glib tongue and disarming mannerisms. And charming smile. Don't forget that rakish flash of teeth that could turn bones to butter.

Why, Ronan almost had her sympathizing with him, and *he* was Mercy's accuser. No, that was too strong a word. Perhaps he only sought to uncover the truth about her parentage, but to what purpose?

Childish laughter brought both of their heads up suddenly, and they swiftly put more distance between them. Marissa and the girls were almost upon the conveyance. Their faces shining, slightly red from heat and exertion, they appeared to have had a romping good time.

"We will continue this conversation later," Ronan said in a low tone for Mercy's ears alone before flashing a welcoming smile as he stood and climbed down to assist them.

That is what I'm afraid of.

"Lord Ronan, I made a friend," Arabelle said, turning to wave at a little dark-haired girl clambering into a curricle several feet away. "Her name is Caroline Bedford."

"Did you now?" Ronan handed her in and then her sister. "Marissa, would you mind terribly sitting beside Miss Feathers so that I might hear all about Arabelle's and Bellamy's adventures?"

Marissa sliced him an odd look but shrugged as he

helped her inside the landau. "Of course not."

"Thank you," he said.

As Marissa settled beside Mercy, she sighed and proceeded to wave her fan vigorously. The slight breeze rustled her bonnet's lavender bow. "Lord, but it's hot. I could bathe in a tub of sorbet right now."

Eyeing Ronan from beneath her lashes as he attentively listened to his animated wards, Mercy's stomach sank. They were bonding with him. It thrilled and grieved her. She wasn't as indispensable as she'd been even a fortnight ago.

Perhaps it was time to consider a position at Balderbrook's Institution for Genteel Ladies.

*Have you ever wondered who went to the effort to see
us secretly placed at Haven House and Academy
for the Enrichment of Young Women? Was it a
guilty parent wishing to secretly provide for us?
A remorseful third party intending to give
us a future? An ashamed relative wanting to
be rid of us? Will any of us ever know who
we really are? In truth, do we want to?*

~ Miss Mercy Feathers during her first year as a
governess in a letter to Miss Chasity Noble

16

Pelandale House Library
25 March 1818
Early afternoon

A woman's soft, quite pleasant singing brought
Ronan up short as he strode past the partially
open library door. He'd just returned home and had a
potentially unpleasant conversation to finish with
Mercy.

Her reaction yesterday had haunted him all day. A
former military man, he recognized fear when he saw
it. And Mercy Feathers was unquestionably afraid.

But of what?

"Not the labor of my hands
"Can fulfill Thy law's demands."

Whoever she was, she was singing *Rock of Ages*. He recognized the hymn from church.

Assuredly it wasn't either of Ronan's sisters. Both admitted to a tin-ear they'd inherited from their father as had he and didn't torture themselves or those around them by professing otherwise. Hence, the Brockmans never hosted musicals and seldom attended them either.

Small favor that.

Even though Ronan couldn't carry a tune in a bucket himself, off-key singing had the same painful effect as talons scraping open the flesh along his spine when he was subjected to such unholy purgatory.

A servant then?

He cocked his head.

"Could my zeal no respite know
"Could my tears forever flow…"

No… Not a servant.

Mercy.

Hadn't father mentioned Mrs. Shepherd was an extremely pious woman? Wouldn't she have instilled such piety in her students as well? It was ironic that such a devout lady and a sister to a bishop had aided in concealing the identities of girls born outside the constraints of marriage—had done so for decades.

"Ballocks. Where is the dashed stupid thing?" Mercy muttered peevishly. "Surely it must be here."

A silent chuckle shook Ronan's chest.

Perhaps not so very pious after all.

Grinning and assuring himself no servant or family member loitered nearby, Ronan slipped closer. He hadn't a qualm about eavesdropping. There was something about Mercy Feathers that didn't quite add up. People who talked to themselves sometimes revealed secrets.

Besides, he still needed to speak with her. He had intended to finish their discussion after the girls' morning lessons. Mercy and his wards typically took a break late morning for a spot of exercise and then biscuits and tea before music instruction.

He'd joined them once, demonstrating his skills on the pianoforte. Mercy hadn't been able to disguise her surprise or a tell-tale blush when he began playing *Greensleeves* while giving her a highly inappropriate, smoldering look.

Instead, today before breaking his fast, Ronan had been summoned to the shipping office regarding an insurance matter that needed his prompt attention prior to *The Arcturus* weighing anchor on the evening tide. Back to America by way of the Caribbean and Cuba—without him.

This was the first voyage he would miss since investing in the ship. In truth, Ronan expected to be more troubled about that disruption than he was. He wasn't positive his lack of distress was a good thing either.

His conscience might've been assuaged if his lack of angst could've been attributed solely to a wish to stay near Arabelle and Bellamy. However, their enigmatic governess proved as much an allure as his wards' wellbeing did. More if he were perfectly candid, though he could not pinpoint exactly what it was about Mercy that held him in thrall.

Yes, she was lovely with those green, green eyes and that curtain of blonde hair with its ribbons of fire. Her womanly figure was everything a man might desire. Yet she never used her feminine attributes to manipulate. She possessed a shrewd, intelligent mind, a keen wit, and exercised discretion and self-control. Furthermore, Mercy was kind, honest, and patient.

However, Ronan rather thought it was her fiery independence he admired most. Her fortitude and resilience. She was unlike any woman he'd ever met, and the more he grew to know her, the more he wanted to know *her*. To know everything about her.

Ronan wasn't in the habit of repining about females but found his mind returning to the governess numerous times throughout the day and night. Wondering what she was doing that very moment. If she'd enjoyed her day. If she was enjoying London.

And…what her worries and fears were.

Didn't Mercy want to know her origins?

Want to know who her parents were…are? If they were still alive?

He pulled his ear and nudged the door open

another two inches with his boot toe.

Would *he* want to know?

Ronan supposed that would depend upon why he'd been cast aside and how much his life, as well as others, would be disrupted by the knowledge.

The females at Haven House and Academy for the Enrichment of Young Women weren't exactly foundlings. What Hester Shepherd charged for her silence and absolute discretion was nearly criminal, according to Father. And that the facility was always full spoke to how much the establishment was sought after by those who could afford her fee.

No wonder.

There was no shortage of illegitimate progeny amongst the upper ten thousand.

Was there an equivalent institution for unwanted sons?

Likely there was.

A sour taste filled his mouth. Those were the children who were cared for. Many more, most of the lower classes, roamed London's streets, filthy, hungry, and without hope.

Haven House and Academy for the Enrichment of Young Women wasn't a well-kept secret, Ronan had learned after a few discreet questions. Neither was the place openly discussed. Yes, the *haute ton* knew of the facility, and yet not a single person he'd spoken with revealed how they'd come by that knowledge.

Indeed, there were lots and lots of proverbial

skeletons in elite closets.

One thing was for sure. No adverts were needed to keep the *foundling home* operating. There were an abundance of clients—and most, he would wager, were members of the *ton* or, at the very least, well-heeled and influential individuals.

Mercy's lilting singing had turned to humming, interrupted intermittently by a mumbled word or two.

Where, pray tell, were Bellamy and Arabelle?

Not that Ronan was genuinely concerned.

By no means was Mercy negligent in her duties. If anything, she was too diligent.

He doubted she'd take a second for herself on her own accord.

Arms folded and one shoulder propped against the doorjamb, Ronan unabashedly took in a delicately turned ankle as the hem of Mercy's navy-blue gown lifted.

"It must be here somewhere," she said, a tinge of impatience in her tone. "I should think a nobleman's house would have some sort of peerage lineage…"

Mercy's words were unintelligible as she reached out and grasped a book high above her head. Straining to reach what must be a seldom read volume, given its inconvenient placement on an upper shelf, she balanced on her toes atop a sliding ladder.

"Aha!" She released a soft, triumphant cry. "I knew it. And not just one volume, but annual editions too. Thank the Lord."

She giggled, her unfettered glee adorable and contagious.

Ronan found himself grinning widely just because she was so giddy. Although what she'd discovered to cause such joy, Ronan couldn't imagine.

By now, he'd advanced inside the library, a trifle worried she was so high up the ladder.

So absorbed in her task, Mercy hadn't realized she was no longer alone.

The late afternoon sun spilled through the round stained glass window at the top of the library's far wall, bathing her in an ethereal glow. Her red-blond curls shone, the gold and reddish rays from the window creating a halo around her head.

Ronan's breath held suspended.

He was afraid to breathe or blink—to do anything to ruin this magical moment. *God above*. She was utterly radiant—stunning—and his heart pitched into a juddery rhythm as unexpected emotion tightened his throat, warming him to his gut as if he'd taken a hefty gulp of whisky.

Swallowing hard, he remained unmoving, unblinking, simply taking her in.

Mercy brushed away a clingy cobweb and a fine coating of dust, seemingly unaffected by the grime or the telltale sign a hairy, eight-legged creature had once roamed the shelves she explored. There was an excellent likelihood its descendants yet crawled about the neglected tomes.

Ronan couldn't fault the maids for not scaling the walls and dusting the uppermost shelves. They weren't hired as acrobats or expected to risk harm to themselves to ensure a few never read books were dust free.

"Debrett's Peerage, Baronetage, and Knightage, Revised by the Nobility 1800," Mercy read aloud. Stitching her brows together and her plump lips slightly pursed, she inspected the neat row of nearly identical books above her once more.

"Not, 1800, I don't think. Perhaps 1794 or 1795?"

She sounded doubtful. Unsure.

Sliding the book back in place, she pulled out three more. "I'll just have to start here, I suppose. Unless there's a copy of an *Essential Guide to the Peerage* or *Almanach de Gotha* too."

Holding the trio of books against her chest with one arm, she ascended another rung and leaned to the right, inspecting the books.

Devil it.

Was she trying to kill herself?

In a thrice, Ronan reached the base of the ladder. "What do you think you are doing?"

A startled yelp escaped Mercy. She wobbled unsteadily and dropped the books to clutch at the ladder. They tumbled downward, one nearly cracking Ronan atop his head.

"Good Lord, you scared the crabgrass out of me, Ronan," she said shakily, her face chalky white. "I nearly fell."

"I'm sorry, Mercy. I ought to have warned you." He eyed the abused books. "If it's any consolation, you almost split my skull with the 1795 edition."

Her eyes went round, and a little soft "Oh," part-sigh, part-exclamation, passed her lips.

"I'm sorry, Ronan."

He shrugged. "It was my own fault."

"Are the books all right?" She chewed her lower lip, worry creasing her brow.

Ronan gathered the books and stacked them on a nearby round rosewood table where a large Cary's celestial globe took center stage. "I don't think they are any worse for the accident."

One had a slightly bent corner, but she needn't fret about that. How often did anyone read *Debrett's*? Likely, a new edition arrived every year and was promptly relegated to a topmost shelf without ever having the cover cracked open.

Who wanted to read list after list of peers every blasted year?

Ronan put a hand on the ladder's side rails. "Come down now. I'll hold the ladder steady."

A white line yet bracketing her mouth, Mercy nodded and descended. When her feet were level with his chest, she muttered. "I can finish on my own, thank you."

Ronan stepped away, but not too far in case she lost her balance again. What would've happened if she'd done so when no one was here?

200

Once she was standing firmly on the floor, he asked again, "What were you doing, and please don't try to convince me those are for lessons." He flicked his fingers toward the imposing books. "Even my stodgy tutors didn't require me to memorize aristocratic lineages."

"No, of course not." Color flamed across Mercy's cheeks. "I did hope to find a copy of *Robinson Crusoe* to read to the girls. They enjoy adventures for our story time before bed."

So she read to them each night even though they were capable of reading themselves. Not a duty but a choice because she loved Arabelle and Bellamy. In truth, she was in all ways, except biologically, their mother.

It hadn't escaped Ronan's notice that she hadn't explained why she wanted the volumes of Debrette's peerages.

One hand clasped to his nape and the other resting on his hip, he glanced around, having no idea where such a book as *Robinson Crusoe* might be. "I can ask Sturges if the library contains *Robinson Crusoe*. He might know."

"Thank you." The smile bending Mercy's mouth was self-conscious.

"Where are Arabelle and Bellamy?" Ronan asked, mindful to keep his tone casual and not accusing.

"Lady Trentholm took them and your sisters to the Countess of Hurtley's for tea this afternoon. I believe the countess has granddaughters near in age to the girls." Another smile tipped Mercy's mouth upward, and happiness made her eyes shine. "They are already making friends. Both have been invited to numerous homes."

"Excellent," Ronan said with a swift glance to the ormolu and green marble mantel clock. Mother and the girls wouldn't be home for at least an hour. He and Mercy could finish their discussion from yesterday. Or rather, make a decision about what to do regarding her elusive origins.

In the hours since they left Gunter's, Ronan had thought long and hard about what Mercy had said.

"Our parents' sins must cast a shadow of shame upon us and smudge our reputations, making us less deserving? Less worthy?"

He'd been an unmitigated boor, a pompous prig no better than the judgmental toffs who turned their noses up at those of a lower station.

Who were they to judge?

Who was *he?*

Let he who is without sin cast the first stone.

Ronan had no idea what fusty recess of his mind that line had come from. He'd never memorized scripture nor called upon the Lord regularly. Besides, Mercy had not sinned. Perhaps her parents had, but she was undeserving of society's censure.

"Mercy, please have a seat." Ronan indicated the blue-striped mahogany scroll-end sofa situated before the unlit fireplace. "I have something to discuss with you."

She glanced up at him questioningly, then veered her attention to the open door.

"Just a moment." It only took Ronan a few seconds to shut the door. "I think it better to ensure no one overhears us."

Giving another stiff nod, she gingerly sank onto the sofa.

Ronan took a seat a few inches away. He looked pointedly at the books she placed on the side table before she sat down. "Are you trying to discover who your family is?"

She darted her tongue out and wet her lower lip.

He envied that tongue for the privilege of tasting her sweet mouth.

"I…" Pink blossomed across Mercy's cheeks, and she cleared her throat. "That is, your sister mentioned Lady Amhurst and that her ladyship was related to a duke. I thought perhaps, given the resemblance Lady Corinna suggested I have to Lady Amhurst…" She bit her lower lip. "I know it's presumptuous of me and far-reaching." She sighed and wilted a little. "I don't know what I'm thinking."

Ronan knew full well. She wanted to discover if she had any family.

And it wasn't so far-reaching considering Adelhied Tyndal, Lady Amhurst, was the Duke of Featherstone's daughter. Mother had revealed that tidbit last evening. It was highly improbable that Mercy's surname, Feathers, was eerily close to the duke's title.

Mrs. Hester Shepherd hadn't been quite as diligent as she professed.

Of a sudden, Ronan remembered Lady Amhurst clearly. It had been at the Rothingham's ball three years ago. She'd arrived with two of her sons. Nice chaps, if a bit wet behind the ears.

Her husband had died the previous year, and she'd just come out of mourning.

"I will help you find your family if you like," he said, emotion making the words oddly thick upon his tongue.

Mercy's mouth parted, and her gaze collided with his. "You will?"

Breathless. Astonished. Full of hope.

"But you must know they won't likely acknowledge you," Ronan said, unwilling to lead her on and cause her more hurt.

He wrapped a strawberry-blonde tendril around his finger that had fled the neat knot at the back of her head. He gave a slight tug before releasing the strand. It had been every bit as silky as he'd imagined.

"It could, likely *will*, stir a scandal, Mercy. Are you prepared for the consequences? The *ton* can be brutal, feral even."

She shook her head, that errant wisp of hair swaying temptingly.

"I understand your concern for your family and Arabelle and Bellamy," Mercy said, a thread of urgency and sincerity tingeing her voice. "I give my word that should I discover my parentage, I won't contact anyone. What would be the point?"

Sadness turned the edges of her mouth downward, and Ronan wanted to kiss each corner until she smiled once more.

She smoothed the dark fabric of her gown over her lap, her gaze focused on her shoes. "If they wanted me to be a part of their lives, they would not have shunted me off to Haven House and Academy for the Enrichment of Young Women when I was less than four-and-twenty hours old."

Ronan hid a wince, even as his heart wrenched for her.

That soon?

"I suspect, given the reactions you've caused since arriving in London, word might've already reached them," he said, choosing his words with care.

Mother had insinuated as much. "Ronan, Miss Feathers's features are striking enough and similar enough to Lady Amhurst's that whispers are bound to reach Adelhied's ears. In fact, she is already making discreet inquiries. The situation is…precarious."

There wasn't much chatter the Marchioness of Trentholm wasn't aware of buzzing about in the elite drawing rooms she frequented.

Putting his bent forefinger beneath Mercy's chin,

Ronan edged her stubborn little chin upward. She, however, displayed that tenacity he adored and steadfastly kept her gaze downcast.

"I know," she murmured. "I've thought of naught else. I've worried about what that means for your family and the girls. I won't bring disgrace upon you, though I don't know what I can do to prevent speculation."

"Because of that, Mercy, last night I took it upon myself to inform my parents that I believe it would be beneficial for all of us to know exactly what we are up against. They agree with me wholeheartedly."

She looked up then, a sheen of tears shining in her green eyes.

"Do you know what it is like, Ronan, to grow up and know you weren't wanted? To never know who your parents were or why they chose to discard you? Mrs. Shepherd did her best to make us feel loved, but she was only one woman. At any given time, there were dozens of girls under her care. Girls whom I love like sisters, but we each knew we were cast-offs."

A tear slipped from the corner of Mercy's eye, and she dashed it away with a bent knuckle. "I detest waterworks," she said with estimable, calm stoicism, blinking away the moisture.

So brave and resilient. So determined to be strong and independent.

But she didn't have to be alone anymore. Didn't have to take every burden upon her slender shoulders.

Ronan was here to help her now. If only she'd permit him.

"No, Mercy. I don't. I've been very blessed to have a loving family," Ronan admitted frankly. "My stepmother has treated my brothers and me as if we were her offspring, and we love her as if she was our true mother."

Even Sanford for all of his pomposity.

"Her ladyship has done the same with Arabelle and Bellamy." A fragile nascent smile arched Mercy's mouth, but no joy reflected in her eyes. "I am one of the fortunate ones as well, in truth. At least someone cared enough to place me at Haven House and Academy for the Enrichment of Young Women and pay the exorbitant fee for my upbringing and education."

Unable to resist touching her an instant longer, Ronan took her hand in his.

Her inquisitive gaze flew to meet his. However, she didn't pull her hand away. Her fingers were long and slender, not quite as soft as a lady's but not the rough hands of a maid's either.

He cradled her palm in his, running his thumb over the blue vein pulsing at her delicate wrist.

"I want to apologize for my behavior yesterday, Mercy. It was not well done of me at all."

He captured her gaze with his own, willing her not to look away.

She stared at him, vulnerable and uncertain.

"I made you feel inferior and ashamed," he said, emotion catching in his throat and making his words raspy. "That was not my intent, and I must beg your forgiveness."

Mercy furrowed her forehead, then shook her head. "You were right. Protecting Bellamy and Arabelle from any scandal must be our top priority. Honestly, I should leave well enough alone."

"So should I," Ronan murmured, his voice raw and cracked with emotion, an instant before he touched his mouth to hers in an achingly tender kiss.

Their first kiss.

I pray you can forgive me in time, for I love you and do not deliberately cause you pain. However, I also love Isadora. That is the long and the short of it. I love her. I don't care that she makes her living on the stage or that she is a commoner. True love is too precious to be constrained by absurd, antiquated dictates or disregarded as a trivial, passing fancy.

~ Letter to the Marquess and Marchioness of Trentholm from Benjamin Brockman
Posted from Scotland

17

Grosvenor Square
Pelandale House library

Mercy should've pushed Ronan away. She should've jumped to her feet and fled the library. At the very least, she should have scolded him for his impudence. For overstepping the bounds.

But she didn't do any of those practical or logical things.

Sighing, she sank into his embrace, welcoming the merest brush of his mouth grazing hers—back and forth. Back and forth. Back and forth. Intoxicating and seductive.

It was...spectacular. Surreal. Breathtaking.

Mercy floated in a haze while at the same time she'd never felt more vibrant and alive. This union of their lips touched her spirit, and something unfurled within her like a dove opening its wings and taking flight. She felt it, the whoosh, as that nameless thing inside her was set free.

An undefinable *something,* she wasn't even aware had been imprisoned.

This was more than a mere kiss. A mere touching of flesh to flesh. Much, *much* more. It made Mercy giddy and dizzy and the tiniest bit off-balance. She shivered, and he tightened his embrace.

"Mercy," Ronan murmured against her lips. "Mercy. Mercy. Mercy."

She understood her name was a supplication and a benediction.

Mercy clung to him, and when Ronan lifted her onto his lap, she melted into his chest, twining her arms about his neck and returning his kiss.

Yes. Oh, yes.

She'd wanted to feel his mouth upon hers for weeks now.

His reverent kisses and lovingly whispered endearments made her feel beautiful and desirable, yes. But they also made her feel as if she were the most precious of priceless treasures.

Unique and exceptional.

All of that with a mere kiss.

"You are a wonder, Mercy," Ronan whispered into her ear, his voice raw and gravelly, husky with primal, masculine need. "I swear...what you do to me. I've never felt this before."

Ronan didn't speak down to her, reminding her of her status as a governess. He spoke to her as his equal, even though he knew the truth of her birth. The rarity of his kindness and decency struck her heart. In that instant, that piece became his forever and always.

Mercy suspected the first piece of her vulnerable heart had landed beside his glossy boots that night in the study when he'd drawn her into his arms and soothed her sobs with light caresses and softly murmured assurances.

How could this be wrong?

This feeling burgeoning inside her for this honorable man?

This coming together as if the Almighty had designed them for this very thing.

Had He?

Mercy wanted more.

More of Ronan.

More of them.

Mercy wanted...*God above*...she actually wanted to know Ronan in the way only a man and a woman can really know one another, to be one flesh with him in the Biblical sense.

That's what your mother thought too.

Was it?

Had her mother been seduced by a charming rapscallion? One who made her forget everything but the sensation of being in his arms?

If so, Mercy could not afford to make the same mistake her mother had. No matter that it might break her heart to reject Ronan. Nevertheless, she'd vowed long ago to never give herself to a man outside the sacrament of matrimony.

That thought had the same effect as diving into the Atlantic in February. At once, reason flooded her, and an icy bleakness enshrouded her soul.

"We cannot, Ronan. I'm sorry."

Face averted, she pulled away from his embrace. Sadness assailed her for what could never be.

Mercy had never dreamed a kiss could tilt her world on its axis. Nay, spin it like a child's toy top. Her reaction only confirmed that she was well on her way to losing her heart to Ronan Brockman.

"You've done absolutely nothing to be sorry for, Mercy." Ronan scraped a hand through his sun-streaked hair, his expression a contradictory mixture of regret and confusion. "It is I who should be begging for your forgiveness. Please believe me when I tell you I hadn't intended to kiss you."

Rising, she willed her heightened senses to return to a semblance of normal. To do that, she needed to put distance between them. She could still feel the heat of his body beckoning her and smell the subtle scent of his cologne.

Sidestepping until she stood a respectable distance away, Mercy tried to ignore the shadow that passed across Ronan's features. Making a pretense of smoothing her skirts, she eyed the closed door.

"This is wrong, Ronan. We both know nothing can come of…"

She waved her hand back and forth, helpless to define what exactly had transpired between them. She didn't want to make more of the kiss than what it was. Likely, he'd kissed dozens of women before her. It wasn't his fault that his kiss was her first.

Sighing, Ronan also stood.

"I agree that wasn't wise timing on my part, but I cannot—won't—regret kissing you, Mercy."

Helplessness enshrouded her at his words. Words that made her want to run into his arms once more and relish the safety and comfort she found in that solid embrace. To nuzzle her face into the hard wall of his chest and stay there forever.

That was nonsensical codswallop—fairy tales and fables. Whimsical fancies.

"Ronan…"

He held his hand up. "Please. Let's not say anything that we might regret, but instead, agree to finish the conversation when the issue of your parentage has been settled."

Because who her parents may or may not be made a difference to him?

If not him, then his family?

Besides, they were making a habit of postponing discussions that needed resolutions. Procrastinating served no one well. Mercy bit her lip, her heart and mind wrestling for dominance.

No. This must be resolved now. Delaying would only lead to misunderstandings, confusion, and even awkwardness between them. She couldn't bear the latter.

She collected her tattered dignity. "Ronan, I think—"

"Ronan?" Lord Trentholm thundered in the corridor, his voice rising an octave on the last syllable.

For one horrible heartbeat, she feared she and Ronan had been found out, but then the marquess yelled again.

"Where are you, Ronan?" The marquess actually shouted for his son. "Sturges. Where is my son?"

What in the world?

His lordship had never raised his voice above a well-modulated tenor that she was aware of. Always impeccably in control, he used his facial expressions to convey his emotions. One arch look was enough to send servants scurrying in every direction.

"Ronan?" Mercy exchanged a bewildered glance with Ronan.

He lifted a shoulder in an I-have-no-idea motion. "I am clueless about what is going on."

"Ronan!" The marquess's voice reverberated off the ceiling.

Brow furrowed in consternation, Ronan strode to the door. Before he could open it, the panel swung open to reveal a highly agitated Lord Trentholm and his eldest son, Sanford, the Earl of Renshaw. The men plowed into the room, raking their gazes over the occupants and then searching the corners as well.

What were they looking for?

"Father?" Ronan angled his head inquisitively, his tone cautious. "What has you in such a dust-up?"

Cheeks ruddy, Lord Trentholm furiously waved a creased paper in the air as he stomped farther into the library. "Benjamin has eloped to Scotland! Eloped, I say. Two days ago."

"Eloped?" Ronan parroted, looking to his brother for clarification. "Benjamin has eloped?" he asked incredulously. "Blast. I didn't think—"

"With an *actress* or a stage performer of some sort," the earl sneered, his lip curling almost ferally. The icy disdain in his voice would've frozen the River Medway in August. "A commoner, and if the gossips are to be credited, the by-blow of a courtesan to boot."

The earl slapped his fist into his palm, cursing beneath his breath.

Mercy had no idea he held the lower classes in such contempt. It wasn't uncommon, of course. But Ronan never had, and she'd mistakenly believed...

No. That wasn't true.

She knew Ronan was a rarity amongst his peers. That was one of the things she loved about him.

Talking animatedly, their voices low and urgent, the trio converged in the center of the room. An occasional curse filtered Mercy's way and several more withering remarks directed at Lord Benjamin's new wife—all delivered in scathing tones by Lord Renshaw—as well.

Seemingly forgotten, Mercy gathered the books she'd taken such pains to find, then edged toward the door. This assuredly was not a discussion meant for a servant's ears. Besides, the girls were due home any time.

"Why didn't he say anything?" the marquess asked, hurt riddling his question. "If he loved the girl, why did he keep her identity a secret?"

"He mentioned her to me recently," Ronan confessed. His back was to her, his hands braced on his narrow hips. "I didn't think the relationship had become so serious."

"And you didn't think to inform me or your mother of something so important?" his father demanded.

Drawing himself up, Ronan faced the irate marquess.

"Benjamin is an adult, and therefore is capable of knowing his own mind and heart, Father. He also asked me to keep his confidence. It was not my place to say anything to you." He cut his fuming brother a speaking glance. "Or anyone else, for that matter."

"Never has the Brockman lineage been tainted

with a commoner's blood," Lord Renshaw spat. "Let alone with a baseborn's and a trollop's."

Mercy winced inwardly, feeling each harshly spoken word as if struck by the verbal blows. The earl might not be directing them toward her, but she felt them as if he had.

Perhaps guilt about kissing Ronan accounted for her reaction. She had no doubt if Lord Renshaw had come upon her and Ronan in an embrace, she would, indeed, be the target of his wrath at this moment.

The marquess, looking very much like he'd taken a blow to the gut, brushed a hand over his forehead and gazed out the window. He wasn't as angry as he was wounded, she decided. He was a man who cared deeply for his family, and his son's eloping struck a painful blow.

Mercy sincerely prayed it didn't cause a rift between father and son.

"I cannot conceive it," Lord Renshaw ranted. "A common slut now bears the Brockman name."

"Sanford," Ronan bit out, leveling his brother a stern shut-your-mouth glare. "There is a lady present."

The earl blinked, and as if slightly dazed, turned his attention to Mercy. His dark brown eyes narrowing, then narrowing further, he looked between her and Ronan. "Why *is* Miss Feathers ensconced in the library with you with the door shut?"

Accusation and insinuation fairly dripped from his voice.

Mercy opened her mouth to reply, but Ronan quelled her with a swift, silencing glance which seemed to say "Let me handle him."

By all means.

She'd rather not have to explain to the irrational man why his suspicions were not well-founded when, in truth, they were spot on.

"I don't like your tone of voice, *Brother*." Glaring daggers, Ronan crossed his arms. "But as you believe you have a right to know why I was having a private discussion with *my* wards' governess, which is my right, by the by, I shall elucidate. Miss Feathers sought my advice on where she might locate a few books she thought Arabelle and Bellamy might be interested in."

The earl deflated to half-sail but still blustered about. "It's not seemly."

"Stuff and rot, Sanford," Lord Trentholm interjected, his focus now fixed on the paper he held. Several deep furrows lined his brow as he studied the words. "Miss Feathers is a servant. Those strictures don't apply to domestics."

And there it was.

The marquess also deemed her as inferior, unheeded, and discounted.

The elite didn't see or hear their servants, much less care about their feelings. What was perhaps more galling wasn't that they were overlooked and ignored. No, it was that servants were all but invisible—objects no more noticeable than a carpet or a clock or a chair.

That truth had never rankled Mercy before, so why should it now, she couldn't fathom.

"I'll excuse myself," she said, retreating into her training. Invisible was good. You couldn't get in trouble if you were overlooked.

Dipping a shallow curtsy and clutching the books to her chest, she made for the door. Never had she been so eager to escape a library. And she'd never be able to look at the Earl of Renshaw again without thinking him a self-important, judgmental jackanape.

Well, that wasn't *exactly* what she was thinking about him. However, even she couldn't acknowledge such uncharitable, low-minded insults to his character.

Ronan sent her a reassuring smile.

No sooner had she reached the threshold than Lady Trentholm came sailing down the corridor, still wearing her raspberry red redingote and matching bonnet. She was in a fine frenzy, her cheeks flushed and blue eyes unnaturally bright.

"Ah, there you are," she said tightly while giving several short, tense nods. The angles of her face stood out in contrast to her usually serene expression. "We have a situation."

*For more years than I care to count, I've
concealed the identities of the girls entrusted
to my care. Nonetheless, I've not been entirely
benevolent. I have broken my solemn oath of
confidentiality. I was angry at the elites who so easily
tossed their offspring aside. I gave each girl a surname
that hinted at her identity as well as a different spelling
of my own surname: Shepard rather than Shepherd.
It was vain and imprudent. Foolish. Judgmental. Now,
for the first time, I fear that one of my dear girls will
suffer for my temerity. She's been found out, and I
dread the consequences for her. Hence, I have decided
to sell Haven House and Academy for the Enrichment
of Young Women. I cannot carry the burden for
these girls any longer, dear brother
May our Lord forgive me.*

~ Mrs. Hester Shepherd in a letter to her brother, the
Bishop of Coventry

18

Just outside Pelandale House library

Time stopped. Mercy's stomach tumbled to her
toes, and fear nipped with sharp, jagged teeth.

Had something happened to one of the girls?

"Is everything all right with Bellamy and

Arabelle?" Mercy asked while her heart fluttered about behind her breastbone like a swarm of butterflies.

"Yes. Yes. They are fine." Behind her mother, Corrina rushed along, though she whipped her sky-blue bonnet off as she went. If her tense countenance were any indication, she was nearly as worked up as the marchioness.

"Marissa has taken Bellamy and Arabelle to the nursery," Corinna offered by way of consolation as she drew off her gloves.

Thank goodness.

A bit of tension eased from Mercy.

Whatever the *situation* was that Lady Trentholm referred to and which had her in an uncharacteristic dither must be one she meant to speak with her sons and husband about.

Mercy curtsied again, eager to see Bellamy and Arabelle and ask them about their day.

Who was she kidding?

She was desperate to put as much distance as she could between herself and the dramatics on display behind her in the library. Or perhaps the new histrionics about to play out. In any event, she preferred to be far away from both.

"My lady. Lady Corinna." Mercy dipped her head and made to keep going, but Lady Trentholm placed her gloved hand on Mercy's arm, staying her. Mercy stared mutely at the delicate pink flowers embroidered on the soft leather.

"Miss Feathers, I need to speak to you at once," her ladyship said in an odd, stilted tone.

Mercy winged her gaze to Corinna, asking a silent question.

Even the vivacious Corinna was subdued and slightly pale. She averted her gaze and gave a little helpless shrug.

Mercy bit the corner of her lower lip.

That could not bode well.

Taking Mercy by the elbow, the marchioness guided her back into the dratted library. The three quarreling men stopped at once upon seeing her ladyship.

Lord Trentholm swiftly crossed the distance to his visibly shaken wife and kissed her cheek. "My dear. I'm afraid I have distressing news."

"You've already heard?" Corinna asked in astonishment, her blue eyes wide with shock. "How is that possible? We've only just heard ourselves."

Mercy sought Ronan from across the room.

His brown-eyed gaze touched her, soothing and encouraging.

The marchioness and the marquess spoke simultaneously.

"Benjamin has eloped," he said.

"Lady Amhurst has come down to town," she blurted. "Word has it she is here to meet Miss Feathers."

The room stopped.

Everyone ceased to move at the exact same instant. No one even drew a breath for six excruciatingly long *tick-tocks* of the clock.

Then everyone spoke at once.

"What did you say?" Lady Trentholm's mouth went slack, and she clutched her throat, tearing open the fastener. "Benjamin has eloped?"

"Benjamin's married?" This from Corinna.

Ronan's "Why would Lady Amhurst want to meet Mercy?" was nearly drowned out by Lord Renshaw's "By God, everything's gone to Hades in a soup tureen!"

Lord Trentholm's mouth sagged wide open as he gaped, utterly flummoxed. "God's blood. What's this?"

His lordship had cursed in front of ladies. A first, for certain.

He speared Mercy a baffled look. "Lady Amhurst? Miss Feathers?"

Despite the severity of the situation, Mercy felt her lips twitch.

If ever there was a comedy of errors, this was it.

"Come sit down, Mama." Corinna put a supporting arm around her mother and guided her to the sofa Ronan and Mercy had occupied just a few short minutes ago.

A lifetime ago.

She could not regret their kiss, even as she knew it must never happen again.

All solicitousness, the marquess followed his wife and daughter. Once her ladyship had flopped—not sank daintily, but actually plopped down upon the cushion—he took her hand in his and patted it.

"Benjamin eloped?" she repeated, tears pooling in her eyes.

"Yes, to Gretna Green, my dear," he consoled. "He sent a letter. The deed is done. Benjamin is married."

Unmistakable sorrow roughened the last few words.

Because his son had felt he couldn't introduce the woman he loved to his family and had denied them the pleasure of a wedding? Or because the marquess grieved his son's choice of a bride?"

Mayhap both.

"Oh, Benjamin. Why?" whispered her ladyship. She fished around inside her silk reticule, finally pulling forth a lacy scrap of cloth. Sniffling, she dabbed her eyes.

This was one of the times Mercy was grateful servants were invisible. She felt a voyeur, watching a private family moment.

As if he'd spoken her name, she sensed Ronan looking at her. She met his gaze for a fraction. He needed to stop staring at her, or someone would notice.

"Why would he elope?" her ladyship asked the room at large. "The first of my children to marry, and his family wasn't there."

"Because he knew deuced well that we would disapprove. And rightly so," Lord Renshaw put in nastily. "He shackled himself to a lowborn actress."

"There are far worse things than marrying the woman you love, Sanford." Arms folded, Ronan regarded his brother coldly.

"Good for him." Corinna grinned broadly at her infuriated eldest brother.

His brows crashed together at her taunting, and Ronan smothered a chuckle.

"I knew Benjamin had a backbone," Corinna said. She waved a finger at Lord Renshaw. "And you do not speak for me, Sanford. I most heartily approve. Brava for him. I, for one, cannot wait to meet her. She must be something extraordinary to have captured Benjamin's heart."

She earned a black glower from the earl, and Mercy was positive he gnashed his teeth.

Then and there, Mercy decided she did not like Sanford Brockman, Earl of Renshaw, and future Marquess of Trentholm. He was an arrogant, closed-minded, pompous prig. She'd ask God to forgive her for her unkind thoughts later.

Mercy hovered near the doorway, still holding the three volumes of *Debrett's Peerage, Baronetage, and Knightage, Revised by the Nobility*. Perhaps it would've been wiser to leave them here and collect them later. If anyone should see the titles, there might be questions asked she'd just as soon not answer.

"What is this about Lady Amhurst?" Lord Trentholm asked, remembering his wife's exclamation. "And what has it to do with our Miss Feathers?"

Mercy's ears perked up despite herself.

"Oh, Arthur." Shaking her head and pressing a palm to her chest, Lady Trentholm released a little moan. As if suddenly remembering she'd asked to speak to Mercy, she searched the room until she found her. "Miss Feathers, please do sit down. I fear you won't want to be standing when I share what I have learned."

Ronan was at Mercy's side in an instant. After taking the books and laying them on a table, he escorted her to a chair kitty-corner to the sofa. Silently, he urged her down onto the plush cushion.

"It's all anyone could speak of at the Countess of Hurtley's today," Lady Trentholm said. "I vow there were two score women in attendance, and everyone, *positively everyone*, spoke on it at length."

Corinna nodded, a grim line replacing her earlier grin. "Indeed, they did. And asked us the most intrusive questions. It was far beyond the pale."

"Mother?" Ronan encouraged. "What has that to do with Miss Feathers?"

Pale and distraught, the marchioness just shook her head and finished drying her tears.

Ronan looked to Corinna, but she also shook her head and actually retreated a step. "'Tis better coming from Mama."

Good heavens.

What could be so cataclysmic that vivacious Corinna was subdued?

Unless…

A niggling suspicion had begun to grow deep inside Mercy. One she couldn't allow to form completely or she'd dissolve into a watering pot. One that was guaranteed to disrupt her life further.

The look Corinna sent Mercy brimmed with compassion and unexpected support.

Dread squeezed Mercy's ribs tighter and tighter until she could scarcely draw in a breath.

"The rumor mills are all abuzz." Lady Trentholm sucked in a long, steadying breath as she untied her bonnet, then lifted it from her head. "Lady Amhurst arrived in London yesterday."

Off came one glove, which her ladyship carefully set upon the sofa's arm.

"Since her arrival, she's been asking about our Miss Feathers," she continued, seemingly oblivious to the people waiting impatiently upon her every word.

"One would think she would direct her questions to us," her husband offered pragmatically.

"One would think," Ronan echoed.

With extraordinarily precise movements, the marchioness removed the second glove, pulling the tip of each finger loose first. "I believe the delicacy of the situation has her…reluctant to impose until she had facts."

Ronan mumbled something under his breath which might very well have been a curse.

By that time, Mercy was ready to scream in frustration. She crossed her ankles and threaded her fingers together.

Patience, she told herself.

Patience is a virtue.

Be patient in affliction.

Bah, how can I be patient at a time like this?

Lady Trentholm brought her gaze up to meet Mercy's, and she realized with a start, the woman had been procrastinating. "She believes you are her daughter, Mercy. She doesn't care who knows it either. She wants to meet you. I expect she shall call tomorrow."

Mercy felt every ounce of blood drain from her face at the same instant Ronan's hand came to rest upon her shoulder. He gave a slight squeeze, and she fought the rush of tears the tender gesture caused. How she wanted to reach up and grip his hand. She needed his sturdy strength at this moment.

She didn't dare, of course.

Lord Renshaw might have an apoplexy or paroxysm.

Lady Trentholm's attention gravitated to Ronan's hand upon Mercy's shoulder, and her eyelids flexed almost imperceptibly. Corinna on the other hand winked, the minx.

So overcome by all that had transpired in the last few moments, Mercy couldn't summon a blush or chagrin for either woman's reaction to Ronan's forwardness.

My mother might be alive.

A peculiar whirring in her ears and a fuzzy sensation in her head made concentrating hard. She wasn't sure whether to rejoice that she might have a mother or weep for fear of the scandal that would taint this household if it were true. Or what that disgrace might do to Bellamy and Arabelle.

Snorting, the Earl of Renshaw threw his hands in the air. "Could any more dishonor befall our family? Now the governess is a baseborn too?"

He spoke about Mercy as if she were a blemished potato or a stool with a broken leg.

"Yes, it could," snapped his father, a hint of irritation and steel in his voice Mercy had never heard before. "Two people who love each other eloping and a young woman reunited with her mother are not the end of the world. The joy of both of those events outweighs any scandal or disgrace. Stop thinking of only your pride for a change, Sanford."

At her father's vehement pronouncement, Corinna grinned and winked at Mercy again.

Mercy truly did adore Corinna.

Ronan gripped her shoulder again.

"Fine," the earl said, stiff with affront. Everything about the man was rigid and uncompromising and prickly pride. "Apparently, as I'm the only Brockman to care a jot about our family's reputation, I shall take my leave."

"You do that," Ronan said. "And while you're at it, I'd suggest counting your many, *many* blessings instead of focusing on petty matters only you perceive as dire."

"Stow it. I don't need a lecture from you," the Earl of Renshaw bit out. He stomped from the room, slamming the door afterward.

The reverberation of the banged door and the steady ticking of the longcase clock punctuated the awkward silence.

"I indulged him when his mother died," muttered the marquess, rubbing his third and fourth fingers across his forehead. "I should've taken him down several pegs when he was a lad."

"You've been a good father, Arthur," his wife consoled. "You are not to blame."

The humming in Mercy's ears grew louder. Swallowing, she blinked several times, attempting to dispel the myriad of tiny black spots dancing before her eyes.

"I beg your pardon," she mumbled, gaining her feet with considerable effort. "I am not feeling at all well."

Swaying, she reached out blindly.

"Ronan, she's going to swoon," Corinna cried.

"I'm sorry…" And then Mercy was falling. Just before she lost consciousness, ironlike arms caught her to a muscular chest.

"I have you," whispered a tender voice into her hair.

*I shall call promptly upon my arrival in London.
Please do not attempt to avoid this long-overdue
Confrontation by pretending to not be at home.
What you have done is not only deplorable
and unconscionable, it is criminal. I am
not above notifying the authorities.
I will, at long last, know the truth.*

~ Adelhied, Countess of Amhurst, in a letter to
the Duke and Duchess of Featherstone

19

*Berkeley Square, London
Duke of Featherstone's house
half of five o'clock
25 March 1818*

Nothing had changed.
Everything had changed.
*I might have a daughter. My baby mightn't have
died.*

A parade of emotions marched through Adelhied
Tyndal, Countess of Amhurst, and she pressed both
palms against her hectic stomach.

Joy, fear, grief, and anger.

Fury unlike any she had ever known. Far
surpassing the rage she'd felt for Amhurst's

philandering and whoring. Or the seething wrath toward her parents for ensuring Charles Abott was sent to the front lines during The War of the First Coalition.

They'd all but pulled the trigger of the gun themselves that had taken his young life.

How the Duke and Duchess of Featherstone had scurried to annul her marriage to Charles. The union they'd arranged decades before with Armond Tyndal, Earl of Amhurst, must take place at all cost.

Adelhied could only imagine the people her parents must've bribed. Even so-called pious men of the cloth. For the annulment had been granted in an unheard-of seven weeks.

A mere seven weeks after her beloved Charles had given his life, they dared to erase and nullify her marriage to him. Against her wishes, of course. But when had they ever considered her wishes?

Adelhied laughed aloud, the scraping sound caustic and bitter to her own ears.

How furious Father and Mother had been to learn she carried Charles's child after the annulment. Adelhied had hidden the pregnancy for as long as she could for fear they'd harm the baby or force a miscarriage. She'd learned just how conniving and devious her parents were, and her genuine heartbreak over Charles's death gave her a reason to isolate herself.

She'd been a full six months along before they learned the truth, and then they were forced to keep her condition a secret. After all, her parents had made certain she wasn't married any longer. Now they had an unwed daughter, heavy with child.

The irony brought an arch smile to her mouth.

Even those two spawns of Satan couldn't out scheme the devil.

Trailing a finger over the carved mahogany back of the settee, Adelhied thought back to the last time she'd seen either of her parents. It had been over four-and-twenty years since she'd seen or spoken to the Duke and Duchess of Featherstone. Not since they'd forced her into an arranged marriage to Amhurst.

She'd climbed into the coach after the ceremony and never once looked back.

There was nothing to look back for.

Charles had died during the siege of Toulon. Their daughter had been stillborn.

Everything she'd loved had died. She no longer cared about her future. A future she was determined to shut her callous, unfeeling, heartless parents out of. Every letter from them had been returned unopened. Until, after five years, they'd simply stopped writing.

They'd made their miserable beds. They could blasted well lie in them.

Now, all of these years later, gossip brought Adelhied to the house she'd vowed never to set foot in again. A rumor that a woman who looked just like Adelhied had been seen in London. A woman with red-blond hair, unusual green eyes, and in her early twenties.

Four-and-twenty, to be precise.

Adelhied's one-time good friend, Rosemond Lancaster, now Baroness of Turlock, had written Adelhied. She'd seen the young woman eating an ice outside of Gunter's Tea Shop in the company of Ronan Brockman, son of the Marquess of Trentholm.

Adelhied knew the Brockmans, of course. She also knew the Marquess and Marchioness of Trentholm. While Adelhied had spurned her parents these many years, she wasn't so imprudent as to rebuff *le beau monde* entirely.

It was a simple matter—a few coins in an overworked servant's palm—to learn which assemblies the Featherstones were invited to and avoid them. To always send a maid ahead into shops to ensure Mother wasn't there ahead of her. To avoid the parks, museums, tea shops, and theaters she knew her parents favored.

Today, however, Adelhied would see her parents face to face.

By all that was holy, she would have her answers.

Her three sons had offered to accompany her, but she'd declined. They were good men. Decent men. Men of integrity and honor.

She'd seen to that by keeping them in the country as much as possible and forbidding any association with her parents. Or her deceased husband's licentious cronies. They'd attended church and country gatherings.

Rather than attend Eton or Harrow, where most boys of station received their educations, Walter, Ronald, and Godwin had been educated by private tutors. Instead of attending Oxford or Cambridge, they'd gone to university in Edinburgh.

Having a Scottish ducal grandfather had eased that pathway.

However, as much as Adelhied would've loved to have their support, she needed to do this on her own. To slay the dragon that had haunted her all of these years. To face the cold-hearted parents who'd bullied and manipulated her until she had cut them from her life.

A small smile played around the edges of her mouth as she examined the portrait of her mother still residing in the place of honor over the fireplace. She'd always been as unfeeling and emotionless as her husband.

In fact, she'd been the one to tell Adelhied, succinctly and without a hint of compassion or sorrow, that her daughter had been born dead.

Had it all been a carefully concocted lie?

Had the midwife been bribed?

Where had her daughter been all of these years?

How could her own parents do that to her?

Adelhied's heart convulsed with renewed pain. She shoved a gloved fist in her mouth to silence the primal moan rising to her lips. Hatred like she'd never known burned in her veins, fueling her wrath, and she hungered for vengeance.

It had been a difficult birth. She'd floated in and out of consciousness. Afterward, Adelhied had been half out of her mind with grief for weeks.

If her parents had lied to her...

If her beloved daughter had lived, by God, Adelhied would see that they paid for their treachery. The annulment should never have been granted because she had been pregnant.

Another glance to the mantel clock revealed thirty minutes had passed since Burrows had escorted her to the drawing room. She hadn't been offered so much as a cup of tea. Likely Burrows was afraid of earning his employers' disapproval.

Just as she crossed the room to yank the bell-pull, the door opened, and her aged parents shuffled into the room arm in arm. Father leaned on a silver-tipped cane, barely resembling the man she remembered.

Shock held her momentarily frozen in place, unable to speak.

Time had not been kind to the Duke and Duchess of Featherstone. Both were thin, wizened, and hunched over. Nevertheless, the unmistakable glint of haughty superiority they'd always borne still shone in their rheumy eyes.

Burrows, the butler for the last four decades, followed them into the drawing room. "Shall I bring tea?"

Now he'd offer tea?

He'd always been a sycophantic coward.

The duchess looked to Adelhied and raised a white eyebrow. "Will you be staying for tea?"

Pity stabbed Adelhied at the desperation in her mother's eyes, and her heart buckled. She would not be like them. Vindictive and vengeful. Besides, she hadn't eaten or drunk anything since breaking her fast this morning.

Adelhied had spent the afternoon inquiring around London about her daughter and hadn't taken the time to eat. Angling her head, she acquiesced. "Tea would be lovely."

Both of her parents exhaled audibly.

Evidently, they'd feared she'd take after them. She had cause to.

She waited until her parents sat upon the settee before she claimed a seat across from them. "I have reason to believe my daughter is alive."

The duke and duchess exchanged a speaking glance.

Adelhied had expected protestations and theatrics. Vehement denials.

She could only conclude they, too, had heard whispers.

"I presume by your silence the rumors are true." A cannonball of emotion formed in her throat. She didn't know whether to laugh or to cry. To shout in jubilation or ring her odious parents a peal.

The duke harumphed and scratched his jaw before

saying, "We only wanted what was best for you—"

Adelhied was on her feet in an instant.

"*Do not,*" she ground out, "justify your contemptible actions on the pretense that what you did was for *my* benefit. I loved Charles. I was of age, and we were legally married. He mightn't have been next in line for a title, but his family was landed gentry, his uncle a viscount."

She drew in a ragged breath, struggling to regain her equanimity and not verbally fillet them with her tongue.

She looked squarely at the duke.

"I know you had him sent to Toulon, Father. You may not have pulled the trigger, but you killed Charles. And if that wasn't evil enough, you took my daughter from me. The only thing I had left of Charles."

The duchess wept softly into a handkerchief she'd procured from her bosom. "You are right, Adelhied. It was wrong. All of it."

"Nonsense, Beatrice." Her father's wiry gray eyebrows wrestled with one another under the force of his fierce scowl. "We only wanted what all aristocratic parents want for their daughters. A brilliant match."

"Parents should want their children's happiness above all else, Father." Adelhied stabbed him with an accusatory glare. "That is what I wanted for my sons. Had any of them chosen to marry outside our station, I would've supported them because I am their mother, and I love them. I would not have ruined their lives. Or caused them unbearable, unending pain."

"Bah. Times have changed," her father grumbled sourly and waved his hand dismissively. "Once upon a time, good daughters did as their parents' bid."

He would put this on her? Blame her?

"Where did you take my daughter?" Adelhied asked curtly, the thin rein she held on her temper becoming more tenuous with each passing minute.

Stilted silence filled the room, spreading like spilled oil to the shadowy corners. The duke jutted his chin out mulishly, his lips clamped tight as an oyster shell.

Obstinate and uncompromising as always.

After releasing a juddery breath, the duchess swallowed.

"It was called Haven House, something or other." Mother gave her husband a sideways glance, an incongruent mixture of defiance and shame creasing her wrinkled face. "I cannot recall the entire name, but your father paid an annual fee. I'm sure we've a record somewhere—"

"Haven House and Academy for the Enrichment of Young Women," Father grumbled. "Cost me a bloody fortune to keep her there. I stopped paying the fee five years ago when the girl took a position as a governess."

"Governess," Adelhied said at the same time he did. Her daughter was Mercy Feathers, a governess in the Trentholms' household. She even had a version of the ducal title as a surname.

Someone had a very droll sense of humor, bless them.

Her daughter was alive.

Sweet God in heaven. Alive.

Tears coursing down her cheeks, Adelhied laughed and hugged herself. "My daughter is alive. My sons will be thrilled."

She was thrilled. Overjoyed. Jubilant. Ecstatic.

"Naturally, you cannot claim her, Adelhied," Father declared with his usual matter-of-fact arrogance. "It wouldn't do at all. The scandal would be monumental."

Did he expect that Adelhied would care?

He shook his head, making the loose skin beneath his jaws shudder like a bloodhound's jowls. "The Featherstone name would be blackened. Your mother and I would be shunned. Cut from Society."

"It's no more than you deserve," she snapped, galled at his selfishness.

Burrows returned with the silver tea service. After setting the laden tray upon the mahogany fold-over tea table between the gold brocade settee and matching chairs, he said, "Will there be anything else, Your Graces?"

Adelhied thought he sent her a sympathetic glance from beneath his lashes. Or perhaps it was guilty and apologetic, for there wasn't any way that at least some of the servants hadn't been aware her daughter had lived. And then was shunted off to some inconspicuous home for foundlings.

In order to keep their positions, they'd become accomplices in a kidnapping.

"No, Burrows. Thank you," Mother said, reaching for the silver pot.

Adelhied waited until the servant left the room before speaking. Though from what she knew about servants, he likely listened just outside the door along with a maid or two, probably a footman, and perhaps even the housekeeper.

"Was my marriage to Charles even annulled?"

Her mother dropped her gaze to the scrap of linen she tortured in her lap. Lips tremulous, she wrung the unfortunate cloth between her hands.

No. Adelhied would bet the redingote off her back that they'd lied about that too.

Had they no fear of the Lord whatsoever?

Were their souls so blackened, they resigned themselves to purgatory?

"Father. Was it?" Adelhied demanded, her voice sharper than she'd ever have dared before. "Was my marriage annulled?"

"No," the duke grunted, his eyebrows snapping together as he scowled. "The deuced church refused."

Reeling from that revelation, Adelhied clutched the chair behind her. Once she was steady on her feet, she lifted her chin. She hadn't been prepared to forgive her parents but had hoped they'd be remorseful or abashed or repentant.

Her mother might harbor a degree of regret, but Father? No, his response heralded his complete lack of contriteness.

"How could you be so evil?" she forced between lips so stiff with ire she could scarcely move them. "You subjected my legitimate daughter to the horrors and cruelties of an unwanted child. Had you any consideration for her? How she would feel, believing she was unwanted?"

"Adelhied...?" Her mother dissolved into tears once more. Her voice frail and tinny, she said, "I am sorry."

From the stubborn set of her father's jaw, he wasn't the least remorseful.

"Be that as it may, Mother. I do not know if I can ever forgive you," Adelhied said, despising the bitterness creeping into her voice and making it strident.

With a final quelling glance to her parents, huddled together like two old cats trying to stay warm, she quit the room.

Perhaps someday she might forgive them, but that wasn't her priority at the moment.

She had correspondences to pen.

The first letter to the Marquess and Marchioness of Trentholm, begging an audience on the morrow.

The other to her long-lost daughter.

Dearest Sister, please reconsider.
I know your position as headmistress has
caused you grief and pain. Regardless, who
else will love those waifs with the same devotion
and care you have? You are the nurturing mother
they lack. Naturally, someday you'll step aside.
However I do not believe that time has yet come.
Please pray upon the matter.

~ The Bishop of Coventry in a letter to his sister,
Mrs. Hester Shepherd

Pelandale House
26 March 1818
Mid-morning

Mercy wandered Pelandale House's small garden, unsure what to do with herself. Fluffer-Muffer walked—more aptly pranced—beside her, mewing softly every little bit.

As always, she wanted Ronan.

So did Mercy, for that matter. But unlike the feline, she knew one didn't always get what one wanted. In all honesty, one seldom did. Life consisted of compromises and concessions—the relinquishing of dreams for the contentment of reality.

Or, if not precisely contentment, then acceptance. To do otherwise led to bitterness and resentment.

"*Meow. Meeooow,*" came the cat's plaintive cry as she rubbed against Mercy's ankle.

"Ronan's not here, Fluffer-Muffer," Mercy informed the miffed cat. "I don't know when he'll be back."

After she'd fainted last night, Ronan had insisted she take the day off from lessons and from overseeing her charges. Marissa and Corinna had taken the girls for an outing to St. James's Park, where they were to meet Cathryn Knighton and her nieces. Afterward, they were to luncheon at the Earl of Towler's.

All of the Brockman males were mysteriously absent—not that Mercy found the Earl of Renshaw's nonappearance objectionable. He was an obnoxious boor.

Lady Trentholm had appointments at the milliners and glovers, according to Sturges. The butler had assessed her with renewed interest this morning when Mercy had come down to break her fast. Undoubtedly, every servant knew the prattle about her and wondered at the veracity of it.

Sometime before Mercy awoke from a fitful slumber, Ronan had slipped a note beneath her bedchamber door. It resided inside her apron pocket, and she slipped a hand in to finger the crisp edge.

He possessed neat, sloping penmanship. The letter

had been much like the man. Bold, decisive, and forthright.

Mercy,

I pray this note finds you fully recovered from yesterday. I've asked my sisters to mind Arabelle and Bellamy for the day. The day is yours to do with as you wish. I have directed the servants to see to your every need.

Enjoy yourself. You deserve it.

I would ask that you not leave Pelandale House, however. I'm sure I don't need to remind you why that would be unwise.

I shall be home this afternoon, and we can talk further then.

Ever Yours.

R.

Ever Yours.

A pipe dream, but a lovely one.

Fluffer-Muffer prowled away to explore beneath a bush where a little brown wren had disappeared.

Mercy wished she was as easily entertained.

In point of fact, she was bored.

Had Mercy dared to defy Ronan and take up a needle, she highly suspected the servants wouldn't have permitted it. In truth, the household ran so efficiently that all of the girls' garments had already been repaired by a maid.

She honestly had nothing to do…other than perusing the volumes of Debrett's, presumably still in the library. The events of the last day had made that research somewhat moot now.

Her suspicions had all but been confirmed.

She couldn't help but marvel at God's purpose and design in all of this.

Could Lady Amhurst honestly be her mother? Why, by all that was holy, was the woman so indiscreet with her inquiries? She must know the tattle her questions were causing.

Shading her eyes with one hand, Mercy took in the scrupulously tended beds.

Not many flowers bloomed this early in the season, but a few sunny daffodils and a rainbow of tulips and hyacinths tipped their faces up to greet the sun. During Mercy's tour of the house and grounds upon her arrival, Mrs. Webber had explained the marchioness had ordered the bulbs directly from Holland.

Reaching a partially secluded nook hedged in on two sides by pink blooming hawthorn bushes, she spied a bench. She'd forgotten about the cozy retreat she'd only caught a swift glance of during her previous tour.

Sighing, she sank onto the black wrought iron bench beneath a matching wrought iron arbor. Rose brambles wove in and out up the sides and covered the top in a verdant tangle. Not even a hint of a rosebud could be found amongst the plethora of green leaves.

It was too early in the season.

What color were the roses when they bloomed?

Mercy thought her ladyship had a fondness for pink and yellow. Perhaps even peach or coral.

Would Mercy still be here to see if her guesses were correct?

What was becoming a familiar pang twinged near her heart.

Stretching her legs out before her, she braced her arms on either side and lifted her face to the sun. Freckles be dashed. She rarely had a chance to enjoy the sunshine. The weather had cooled significantly from the other day, but it was still very pleasant outdoors.

Not as pleasant as Rochester, but quite tolerable, nonetheless.

One of the things Mercy missed the most about country life was the lack of roosters crowing to announce a new day. That and cattle bawling and sheep bleating. She supposed, at heart, she would always be a country girl.

Pulling her legs onto the bench, she laid on her side, her head on a bent elbow. She couldn't recall any other time in her life when she'd had the luxury of resting on a garden bench with no responsibilities.

A few birds—she didn't know what kind except they had redbreasts—darted about the branches of the single cherry blossom tree in the center of a circular mosaic. Their sweet calls carried through the garden, making her smile.

This reminded her of Rochester. Mercy doubted she'd ever prefer the city to the country for all of the amenities London had to offer.

Blinking sleepily, she yawned behind her hand. Goodness, the sun made her drowsy.

She still couldn't believe she'd fainted last night. Mercy had never swooned in her life and to collapse in Ronan's arms in front of his family... She supposed that was better than striking the floor, but humiliation still burned in her veins.

She'd awoken shortly afterward in her chamber, Corinna on one side of the bed and her ladyship on the other, holding a vial of smelling salts beneath Mercy's nose.

Nasty, nasty stuff that.

Mercy promised herself this was the one and only time she would swoon. The fumes of that vile concoction were not to be borne. She vowed she could still smell the ammonia, and her nostrils twitched in remembered affront.

Once she'd come to herself, she realized Ronan stood at the end of the bed, keenly watching her, his arms folded. Concern and speculation glinted in his eyes, as well as something undefinable. An expression deep within his chocolatey brown gaze made her stomach wobbly and her blood hum.

Most discomfiting with his mother and sister watching every nuance on her face.

A blush, very much like the one that had heated her face yesterday evening, bloomed across her cheeks once more.

What must Ronan think of her?

Having a fit of the vapors over a little upset. Well, perhaps more than a *little* upset. A noblewoman believed that Mercy was her daughter. After all of this time, was it possible?

Ronan had bid her good evening once assured she was fine. Unable to help herself, she'd watched as he left the room, leaving the door open behind him until he'd disappeared from sight.

Coming to herself, she'd caught both Corinna and her ladyship regarding her with speculative expressions.

Lady Trentholm had sent her lady's maid to assist Mercy into her plain night rail. Another maid had brought her dinner up a short while later. She'd all but been forbidden to leave her bed until the morning.

Marissa had brought the girls in to say goodnight. They'd refused to go to sleep until they had seen Mercy and were assured she wasn't about to perish. Many hugs and kisses later, they'd been led away, and she'd been left alone to contemplate her fate.

The Trentholms had been inordinately

kind...except for the earl. But that didn't mean they weren't bothered by the undesirable attention that was sure to come their way.

The question that had plagued her since yesterday raised its barbed head.

"What am I to do now?" Shutting her eyes, she whispered, "Do I stay or do I go?"

*Mercy, I hope you shall permit me to call you Mercy.
I am sure this situation is every bit as astounding
and bewildering to you as it is to me. I believed my
daughter had died at birth. I was told she had, you
see. I've since learned she did not, in fact, die. My
daughter was taken to a foundling home, and you
are her. My parents confirmed your identity with
absolute certainty just yesterday. It is a long and
unpleasant story, but I pray you will understand
that I never stopped loving you.*

~ The Countess of Amhurst to her daughter,
Miss Mercy Feathers

21

*Pelandale House gardens
An hour later*

Holding the letter addressed to Mercy that had been
delivered as Ronan arrived home a few minutes
ago, he examined the green wax seal. He had no doubt
who had sent it. Another lay on the hall table addressed
to his parents.

Lady Amhurst had wasted no time in seeking an
audience with Mercy.

He skewed his mouth to the side, uncertain
whether to be relieved or irritated that she'd presumed

Mercy was employed by the Trentholms.

"Where is Miss Feathers?" he asked Sturges.

"I believe she is yet in the gardens, Lord Ronan. While washing the library windows earlier, Penny saw Miss Feathers taking the air. I do not believe she has come indoors yet."

"Thank you, Sturges. Please make sure water for tea is kept heated. We are expecting a guest today, though I am not positive when she will call."

"Lady Amhurst, I presume?" Sturges asked without even the pretense of chagrin.

Of course, the servants knew. Nothing went on in the household they didn't know.

"Yes," Ronan said, nodding. Then promoted by some unnamed devil on his shoulder, he asked, "How did Mrs. Sturges like her cold bath? Did it help her sleep?"

Raising his prominent nose, Sturges sniffed. "She did not favor the immersion in cold water, and I was banished from our bedchamber for a week."

Ronan had the good grace to feel abashed. "Sorry about that, old chap. Perhaps it's only us men who find it beneficial."

"Indeed," the butler replied, his tone as dry as cold ash.

Waving Mercy's letter, Ronan said, "I'll just see that Miss Feathers receives this. I believe she might want to read it before Lady Amhurst's arrival."

Well pleased with himself, he grinned.

He'd made sure Mercy had no responsibilities today. She needed time to recover from her shock and yesterday's upset.

The moment he stepped from the house onto the small terrace, Fluffer-Muffer dashed to his side. Spine arched and chirping little welcoming sounds, she wound herself around his feet.

"Not now, puss. I have another lady whose company I much prefer over yours." Ronan set her inside and swiftly closed the door. Not, however, before she flicked her tail indignantly and leveled him a green-eyed feline glare that promised retaliation.

Hopefully, not another shredded bed pillow.

That cat really was a menace.

It didn't take him long to find Mercy curled up and sound asleep on a garden bench. She hadn't put her hair up today. The glossy golden tresses strewn with their ribbons of bronzes and reds trailed over the wrought-iron seat and onto the grass below. Her peach-tinted bowed lips were slightly parted, the faintest flush upon her smooth cheeks.

The sight of her in repose took Ronan's breath away. He was falling into dizzying sensation, entirely under her spell. What was more, he rejoiced in it. Welcomed the onslaught.

In a heartbeat, an epiphany slammed into him with such might that he nearly staggered backward under the realization.

"I love her."

I love her. I love Mercy.

And it was so right and perfect that Ronan couldn't believe he hadn't recognized his love before now. That the uncertainty, the magnetism, the undefinable feelings, had all pointed toward love.

He knelt beside her, and unable to resist, kissed her velvety cheek, then her soft petal lips.

Her eyelids flickered before slowly opening, and he found himself wading into pools of green. Her sleep-soft gaze went softer still.

"Ronan," she murmured, reaching up to trail a finger over his scar.

Never had any touch been more stirring or reverent. Grasping her hand, he turned the palm to his mouth and placed a long kiss there, putting into that simple gesture everything bubbling inside him. All of the love and adoration and wonder and reverence he felt for this priceless woman.

"I was dreaming of you." Her lips formed a faint smile. "And then here you are."

Ronan ran his fingers through her hair, brushing the strands off her face and shoulder.

"Was it a good dream?" he asked half-jestingly.

A wider smile bending her mouth, she sat up and swung her legs off of the bench. "A lady never dreams and tells."

"Ah, then it must've been a very good dream, indeed," he quipped.

As he sat down beside her, he set the letter on her

254

lap. "This came for you. I thought you might want to open it at once since I believe it's from Lady Amhurst. I have no doubt she will call before the day is out."

He knew for a fact she would. She had told her parents as much.

He and Father had paid a call on the unsuspecting Duke and Duchess of Featherstone this morning at the ungodly hour of ten. The duke, the obstinate old goat, had refused to see them. However, the duchess was another matter.

Her grace had been surprisingly forthcoming. The tale she'd told had raised Ronan's ire and his father's censure. To her credit, the Duchess of Featherstone didn't downplay her part in the unpardonable debacle. Unlike her blighter of a husband, her concern was for her daughter and granddaughter.

She vowed, though it meant social ruination, she'd testify publicly if need be to assure Mercy was granted her rightful position in Society.

Before Ronan and his father took their leave, they had no doubt Mercy was the Featherstones' granddaughter. Adelhied Tyndal, Countess of Amhurst, fully intended to recognize her daughter, come what may.

Ronan couldn't help but respect and admire her for her courage and cocking a snook at the *haut ton*. He fully intended to like the woman on sight that he fervently hoped would be his future mother-in-law.

"I'm not sure I want to read it, Ronan." Mercy

stared at the envelope but didn't pick it up. "I fear it means everything is going to change." Her lower lip trembled, and she attempted a brave, tremulous smile. "I cannot leave the girls."

Or me. You cannot leave me.

He wrapped an arm around her shoulders and brought her near. Speaking into her magnificent hair, he said, "You cannot hide from the truth, Mercy. Better to know, I think, and face whatever is in there."

Carefully, with the forefinger and thumb of his other hand, he nudged her chin until she faced him.

"Look at me, Mercy."

She raised her thick lashes until their gazes meshed.

His spirit fused to hers as surely as if someone had melded them together with a forge.

"Ronan, I…"

"Shh." He placed two fingers over her lips. "Hear me out. I will be with you through whatever happens." He brushed his fingers over her shoulder. "I will not abandon you or forsake you."

Her eyes grew misty. "Why? I've brought scandal upon you."

"Hush. You've done no such thing." Ronan kissed her forehead, then lifted her hand and pressed his lips to each knuckle. "I love you, Mercy. I would spend the rest of my life with you. Have you beside me and help me to raise Arabelle and Bellamy and our own children. To face whatever God brings our way together."

"Oh, Ronan." She touched two fingertips to her mouth, her eyes enormous and luminous. Her gaze dipped to the unopened letter. "You risk much."

He gave her a lazy smile. "Nae. The risk is in not asking you to share my life. To be my wife. I don't think I could bear a future that doesn't include you in my life every day. Will you marry me, Mercy?"

Flicking a finger at the crisp rectangle, he asked, his voice hoarse with emotion, "No matter if that letter brings good news or bad?"

"I want to. Lord knows I want to." She crinkled the letter in her fist. "But what about your family? Your brother?"

She didn't have to clarify which brother she referred to.

"Sanford has no say over my life. My parents want my happiness, and…" He winked. "My sisters are completely besotted with you."

A slow smile curved Mercy's mouth, growing larger and larger. "Then, yes. I will marry you, Ronan. I love you so very much."

He let out a triumphant whoop that startled the poor birds from the flowering cherry tree's branches. "Thank God."

"I tried not to love you. I felt it was wrong." She kissed his scar. "But my headstrong heart wasn't having any of the misgivings my mind was. My heart knew even before I did that we were meant to be together."

"As did mine, my love," Ronan whispered against her mouth.

The letter was temporarily forgotten. Mercy was in his arms, and he showed her with kisses the many ways he loved her.

I am to marry, Chasity.
I honestly didn't think God had ordained
that marriage would be part of my destiny. I was
prepared to spend my life as a spinster. Nonetheless,
come next week, I shall be Mrs. Ronan Brockman. Joy
and I have both found our true loves. I have to believe
that you and our other dear friends will too.

~ Miss Mercy Feathers in a letter to
Miss Chasity Noble

22

Pelandale House drawing room
26 March 1818
Three in the afternoon

Ronan sat beside Mercy on the settee as they awaited Lady Amhurst's imminent arrival. Their usual composed selves once more, his parents occupied the chairs opposite. Corinna and Marissa hadn't yet returned home, which was just as well.

Steam spiraled upward from four cups of tea. No one had taken a drink yet, as if they all waited for Lady Amhurst to arrive. Mercy simply could not think of the woman as her mother yet. It was too surreal and too new.

Unsure what to expect from Lady Amhurst's visit, Mercy was relieved the girls wouldn't be about should things become dramatic. After reading her mother's letter, Mercy didn't think that would be the case. Nevertheless, it was wise to err on the side of caution.

"Father. Mother." Ronan's baritone interrupted her reverie. He took Mercy's hand in his, and his parents exchanged meaningful looks.

He meant to announce their betrothal now?

Before the countess arrived?

"If you mean to tell us Miss Feathers will soon become an official member of our family, Son, you have our blessing." The marquess gathered his wife's hand in his and pressed a kiss to her knuckles. "I pray you are every bit as happy as Rachael and I."

"Indeed," her ladyship said, a pleased smile wreathing her face. "We could not be more delighted to welcome Mercy into the family."

Mercy hadn't expected their immediate acceptance.

Humbled and grateful for their kindness, Mercy managed a throaty, "Thank you, my lord and lady."

"*Tut tut.* None of that," the marchioness admonished gently. "Rachael and Arthur will suffice for now." Another glance passed between her and her husband. "We would be beyond pleased if you called us Mother and Father after your vows are exchanged, unless you wish to begin doing so now."

Tears stung Mercy's eyes.

"Thank you." Ronan's tenor was suspiciously husky as he squeezed her fingers and then entwined them with his.

This was a far warmer acceptance than she'd anticipated. She ought to have trusted Ronan when he assured her his parents, unlike his older brother, didn't care more about social status or position than they did love.

"The Countess of Amhurst," Sturges announced a moment before an elegant woman in a sage green gown of the first tulip of fashion glided into the room.

Ronan and the marquess rose as one.

"Oh my." She came to an abrupt stop several feet inside, her face going pale as chalk. "*Oh my*," she said again, staring unblinkingly at Mercy.

A soft rush of air whooshed through Mercy's parted lips as she slowly stood.

"Good heavens." Rachael looked back and forth between Lady Amhurst and Mercy several times. "The likeness is nothing short of astonishing."

"As if I'm looking into a mirror many years ago," Lady Amhurst managed with a shaky smile.

She came forward then, her hands outstretched.

"Mercy," she said simply.

And then Mercy was in her arms, weeping and laughing and trying to talk. There wasn't a dry eye in the room, not even Sturges, who surreptitiously dabbed at the corner of one eye as he replaced the silver teapot with a fresh pot of tea.

The next several hours passed in a blur.

The four girls came home and were introduced.

Adelhied was invited to stay for dinner, which she eagerly accepted.

Afterward, everyone except Sanford, Bellamy, and Arabelle gathered in the drawing room. Mercy covertly eyed the clock. At half of eight, she said, "Please excuse me for a few moments so that I can tuck the girls in. They sleep better if I do."

Adelhied looked slightly startled but regained her composure with practiced swiftness. "Of course, my dear. It is time I took my leave in any event. I'm sure we'll be seeing a great deal of one another these next few days until arrangements can be made for you to come and live with me."

Mercy jerked in surprise.

What?

She hadn't considered her mother would expect her to move in with her. She also didn't know Mercy and Ronan were betrothed.

"Arthur, let's give them a few moments alone, shall we?" Rachael suggested with the astuteness of an observant woman who wasn't really giving her husband a choice. "It has been an absolute delight, Lady Amhurst."

Arthur bowed. "Good evening. Please call again soon. We are delighted at this turn of events."

"As am I." Smiling, Adelhied speared Mercy a warm glance.

Arm in arm, the Trentholms left the room. At the

door, Rachael turned and gave Ronan an are-you-coming look.

He crooked an eyebrow and flashed one of his engaging smiles as he mouthed, "Go along."

"Your ladyship," Mercy began.

"Please, my dear. I know it is too soon to ask you to call me Mother, but mightn't you at least use my given name?" Adelhied asked, her gaze sweeping lovingly over Mercy.

"I should like that," Mercy said. "Mother?" she tried the unfamiliar word upon her tongue.

Her mother beamed. "Yes, dearest?"

"As much as I wish to spend time with you, I cannot leave Bellamy and Arabelle." Mercy hurriedly explained the reason they were in London to begin with. "I feel responsible for them."

"Lady Amhurst." Ronan placed his arm about Mercy's waist. "Just today, Mercy agreed to be my wife."

Adelhied was silent for several extended seconds, her attention flitting back and forth between Ronan and Mercy. Her expression softened. "I see. Well, then we'll just make other arrangements."

"Thank you for understanding," Mercy said as they walked together toward the door.

"Of course, darling. We will take things slowly." She kissed Mercy on the cheek. "I'm just so grateful to have found you. Your brothers will be overjoyed as well."

"Brothers?" Mercy had brothers?

"Did I forget to mention them? How could I have done?" Adelhied puzzled her brow as Sturges assisted her into her emerald redingote, then handed her the matching bonnet. "Yes, well. There are three, you see. Walter is two-and-twenty, Ronald is twenty, and Godwin is nineteen. They shall adore you, Mercy."

Ronan chuckled behind them. "Mercy, in short order, you will have acquired five brothers and two sisters."

After bidding her mother farewell with a kiss to her cheek, Mercy and Ronan made their way to the nursery. Exhausted from their all-day outing, Arabelle and Bellamy were nearly asleep. A simple kiss upon the forehead followed by "Sweet dreams" sufficed tonight.

A lightness Mercy hadn't ever recalled feeling before engulfed her.

As she stood outside her chamber door, she smiled up into Ronan's face.

He braced one hand upon the door frame and leaned down to sweep his lips across hers.

"I'd prefer a short betrothal if you are of the same mind, my darling."

Standing on her toes, she wrapped her arms around his neck. In an instant, he pulled her tight against him and nuzzled her neck.

The slight bristles of his beard tickled and abraded at the same time.

"I believe," she said, "a short betrothal is an excellent idea indeed."

Balderbrook's Institution for Genteel Ladies
Has hired a new music and dance instructor.
Mr. Terramier comes three days a week, and I
must tell you, it is not a good thing. Mr. Terramier
is Viscount Woolbury's rapscallion grandson,
and he has brought disfavor upon the school
with his rebellious antics. I honestly believe he
only took to teaching to spite his grandfather. The
viscount has threatened to have the school closed.

~ Miss Chasity Noble in a letter to
Miss Purity Mayfield

Kelvingrove Park
Bristol, England
August 1818
Late afternoon

Ronan leaned a shoulder against an oak, waiting for Corinna to hit her ball through the wicket. The orange ball went flying, smacking into Walter Tyndal, Earl of Amhurst's, black ball, sending it pelting down the hillside. It stopped just short of the lake. Well, more of a large pond currently occupied by a half dozen ducks.

Benjamin released a long whistle and saluted Corinna. "Outstanding shot."

Mercy, Isadora, and Miss Knighton clapped in delight.

"Well done, Corinna," Mercy called, grinning.

So far, the females were trumping the males, and masculine egos were beginning to bruise.

Amhurst didn't think Corinna's shot was so terrific as he stalked off toward his ball, grumbling good-naturedly beneath his breath the whole while.

Benjamin took his stance behind the green ball. One eye closed, he took a practice swing.

"Come, darling," Isadora called. "I believe in you."

Benjamin's ball was stuck between the trunk of a tree and a rock. He had about as much chance of getting out of the predicament as snails have of fleeing a wildfire.

"Good thing you do, Isadora," Ronan drawled. "He'll need more than a prayer and a whistle to escape that conundrum."

"Stow it, Ronan," Benjamin groused, his eyes narrowed in concentration.

The weeklong house party was coming to an end, culminating with the grand ball tonight. The guests would return home the day after tomorrow. Sanford had declined to attend as had been his wont since his two brothers had gone off and wed *unsuitable* women.

It mattered not to Sanford that Mercy had never been illegitimate, that she was the granddaughter of a duke, and the sister of an earl. Sanford had lifted his imperious nose and stupidly stated, "Scandal surrounds your wife, Ronan. Much like fish gone bad, the offense to one's sensibilities cannot be ignored."

Sanford had sported a blackened eye for a fortnight after making the egregious error of comparing Ronan's new wife to rotting fish.

Ronan heartily prayed that when Sanford gave his heart—if he still had a heart to give—it would be to a highly inappropriate woman, and he'd be forced to eat a massive serving of humble pie. And Ronan would be there to rub a bit of salt into the wound.

All of Mercy's family was in attendance, as had become their habit. If they weren't at the Brockmans', the Brockmans were at the Tyndals'. Mercy and her mother had grown very close, and Adelhied had struck up a friendship with Rachael as well.

Mercy had even met her grandparents, the Duke and Duchess of Featherstone before they'd retired to the duchy's country seat permanently. *Le beau monde* had not responded kindly to their machinations, and the Featherstones had found Society's doors closed to them. More like slammed in their aristocratic faces.

Mercy, on the other hand, the *haut ton* welcomed with surprising warmth. Ronan had no doubt his parents were partially responsible for his wife's acceptance.

"Her grace's regret for her part in the scheme that separated my mother and I seemed quite genuine, Ronan." Mercy had told him after the encounter with her grandparents. She'd wrinkled her nose and shook her head. "But the duke...He's the worst sort of pompous windbag. He looked me up and down like I was livestock. I do not believe I measured up."

"Never mind that old boor. You are perfection in my eyes," Ronan had whispered in her ear before taking her into his arms and showing her just how perfect she was.

Ronan wiped a bead of perspiration off his forehead as he took in the peaceful surroundings. He'd been so busy with his investments these past years that he'd spent little time in the country. He'd forgotten how much he enjoyed it.

"What has you looking so pensive?" Mercy slipped up beside him and gave him a swift hug.

Smiling down at her, he drew her near. His turn wasn't until after Miss Knighton's. "I was just thinking that I like the country. What would you say to us buying a country estate?"

"Truly?" Mercy's eyes glowed as she peered into his. But then her gorgeous green eyes clouded. "But what about your ship? Your business ventures in America and elsewhere?"

"I'll remain part owner." Ronan tweaked her nose. "Just a less active one. I found that I do not wish to be away from my bride or our daughters. My days of roaming about the world have come to an end. I'd like to settle in the country with my beautiful wife and add a babe or two or five to the nursery."

The others had wandered over a slight knoll and were out of view, though not out of earshot.

"Five babes?" She laughed, then her eyes grew soft. "I should like that above all else, Ronan, though I do enjoy London in the spring."

"Above all else, you say, Madam?" Ronan teased as he drew her deeper into the oak copse bordering the lake.

"Sir, are you attempting to lure me away from the others?" Mercy feigned dismay, although the hilarity in her eyes eschewed any genuine concern.

"Is it working?" Ronan asked, waggling his eyebrows and dipping his head to steal a kiss. "We could get started on filling our nursery."

"We cannot." She shot a worried glance toward the others' voices. "It's scandalous. Besides, I promised our mothers I'd spend a few minutes with them going over the last-minute details for the ball."

"Very well, but you shall not escape without another kiss." Securing her in his arms, Ronan enjoyed a leisurely exploration of Mercy's mouth. This woman who had become his wife three months ago had brought him more joy than he'd ever imagined. She was a loving mother to Bellamy and Arabelle, and he couldn't wait until her belly grew round with his child.

With a good deal of reluctance, he set Mercy from him. "Any more, and I shall have to find an excuse to rush you into the house."

That might prove most awkward.

"Ronan. It's your turn," Benjamin called. "Ronan!"

"Alas, duty calls," he lamented, with an actor's flair for dramatics.

Mercy laughed and gave him a little shove. "Go. We have a lifetime together."

Ronan caught her to him. "I love you, Mercy Brockman."

Her eyes grew soft, and she cupped his face. She'd never once flinched from his scar. "And I love you, my heart."

About the Author

USA Today Bestselling, award-winning author COLLETTE CAMERON® scribbles Scottish and Regency historicals featuring dashing rogues and scoundrels and the intrepid damsels who reform them.Blessed with an overactive and witty muse that won't stop whispering new romantic romps in her ear, she's lived in Oregon her entire life, though she dreams of living in Scotland part-time. A self-confessed Cadbury chocoholic, you'll always find a dash of inspiration and a pinch of humor in her sweet-to-spicy timeless romances®.

Explore **Collette's worlds** at
www.collettecameron.com!

Join her **VIP Reader Club** and **FREE newsletter**.
Giggles guaranteed!

FREE BOOK: Join Collette's The Regency Rose®
VIP Reader Club to get updates on book releases,
cover reveals, contests, and giveaways she reserves
exclusively for email and newsletter followers. Also,
any deals, sales, or special promotions are offered to
club members first. She will not share your name or
email, nor will she spam you.

http://bit.ly/TheRegencyRoseGift

Follow Collette on BookBub
https://www.bookbub.com/authors/collette-cameron

From the Desk of Collette Cameron

Thank you for reading NO LORD FOR THE LADY. This is the second book in my Daughters of Desire (Scandalous Ladies) series. I've waited a very long time to write this sweet inspirational series, which features illegitimate heroines.

Like all the heroines in the series, Mercy Feathers is raised in a foundling home. Those women are also guaranteed training in the profession of their choice. Those choices were limited to the few professions society deemed appropriate for respectable women during the Regency era. Mercy chose to become a governess, even though young, attractive governesses risked much. She was fortunate that her first employer, Lieutenant Masterson, was an honorable man.

As you learned in the story, Ronan isn't the typical aristocrat's son. He enjoys his independence, but as every good hero worth his salt does, Ronan accepts the unforeseen changes that come his way.

I mention some of his closest friends. These are their stories if you are interested in reading them:

Allen Wimpleton—A KISS FOR A ROGUE, The Honorable Rogues Series®

Landry Audsley, Earl of Keyworth—EARL OF

KEYWORTH, Seductive Scoundrels Series

Ewan McTavish, Viscount Sethwick—HIGHLANDER'S HOPE, Castle Brides Series

Jason Steele's story, TWAS THE ROGUE BEFORE CHRISTMAS—out soon.

To stay abreast of the releases of the other books in the Daughters of Desire: Scandalous Ladies Series, you can subscribe to my newsletter (the link is below) or visit my author world at collettecameron.com.

I hope escaping into the romantic past with Ronan and Mercy when times were simpler and chivalry reigned provided you with a pleasant reprieve for a little while.

Hugs,

Collette

Connect with Collette!

Check out her author world:
collettecameron.com
Join her Reader Group:
www.facebook.com/groups/CollettesCheris
Subscribe to her newsletter, receive a FREE Book:
www.signup.collettecameron.com/TheRegencyRoseGift

Made in the USA
Monee, IL
16 June 2021